The
Angel
Carver

for Connie.
warmest wishes,

by Francis Eugene Wood

Fran Eye Wood 2013

Illustrations by Martha Pennington Louis

Published by Tip-of-the-Moon Publishing Company
Farmville, Virginia

Printed by Farmville Printing
Photograph by Daniel Wood

email: fewwords@moonstar.com
website: http://tipofthemoon.com

ISBN: 0-9657047-4-2

For Chris

Note from the Author

The idea of *The Angel Carver* was born in January of 1989 when I came upon a book of poetry published in 1901 by a long-forgotten American poet. Alfred Castner King had been a lover of nature, a man of the mountains and forests who had embraced the beauty of the natural world with his heart and soul. His poems were written after an accident left him blind.

I have read his poems over the years and, at times, have been overwhelmed by the beauty of his words. King's poetry possesses a spirit that reaches through time and beyond the darkness that shrouded the man. Although little is known of this blind poet, I have taken license with him and based the person of Beecher Whitman on what I imagine to be his character.

For the setting of the story, I chose the area around Priest Mountain in Nelson County, Virginia. Many of the places mentioned within these pages exist today, although I have taken some liberties with their history.

The blizzard referred to in the story is, in fact, commonly known as the great snowstorm or blizzard of 1940. The storm, which was centered in Farmville, Virginia, is well documented. My research came from eyewitness accounts and articles printed in the *Farmville Herald* and the *Richmond News Leader* at the time, and available now through the archives at the Longwood College library.

Over the years, I have been afforded the opportunity to work with some of the finest artists in the area, a tradition that I intend to continue. I am proud to have the work of two such artists gracing the cover and inside pages of *The Angel Carver*. Eldridge Bagley's original painting captures the rustic simplicity of Beecher Whitman's cabin, while lending an air of mystery to his craft. The sketches by Martha Pennington Louis are superb and bring life to the images of the mind. It has been a delight and a writer's dream to have worked with these talented individuals.

My thanks go out to Elizabeth Pickett and my aunt, Jeanne Clabough, for their editing skills and encouragement. It is good to share my thoughts with those who understand and appreciate the depths in which the creative spirit dwells.

All my love to my wife, Chris, who coaxed me into the light with my stories, and to my sons, Camden and Daniel, who have been inspirations to me for all of their lives.

I am also grateful to my mother and father for allowing me freedom as a child and for never denying the spirit of a dreamer.

FEW
August 26, 1999

Christmas Eve 1998

Julianna tiptoed across the carpeted floor. A dwindling fire flickered from a brick hearth and gave life to shadows which crept against the high walls of the room. A sparkle from a darkened corner caught the child's eye, and she stopped and looked at where she knew the tree stood. It was massive and its top would have swept the ceiling had it not been cropped and fitted with a star.

"I think it is the largest Christmas tree we've ever brought into the house," her grandfather had said.

And she believed it. It was adorned from top to bottom with the most beautiful decorations. There were red and gold ornaments of all descriptions—little wooden sleds and painted Santas and bells and stars that twinkled. There were shiny objects that jingled and clinked when touched. Angels and birds and a baby in a cradle hung from delicate branches in silent beauty. Down low on the tree Julianna's little sister, Missy, had placed the lopsided snowflake she had made in Sunday school. Their mother's commemorative wedding bell dangled on a branch next to her husband's painted wooden soldier, a memento he had placed on Christmas trees since he was very young. They had all brought their own special ornaments to hang on the great tree. It was a family tradition.

Julianna looked behind her, then stepped over to the hearth. She reached out her hands and felt the warmth from the glowing embers. She bent over and peered up the chimney. The damper was set so that only a small opening appeared. The girl straightened and shook her head. She felt the stockings she and her brother and sister had hung on the mantel earlier. They were empty. She sat down on the hearth and stared into the fireplace, her eyes filling with tears. Absorbed in her thoughts, she raked the fire screen with her finger.

Then a familiar voice spoke her name, "Julianna?" The voice was just above a whisper.

The startled girl turned quickly and focused her eyes on the face of her grandmother. "Gramma," she asked, "what are you doing up so late?"

"I was wondering the same thing about you," her grandmother answered, raising an eyebrow.

Julianna lowered her face and fiddled with the lace on her nightgown. "I couldn't sleep, Gramma."

The woman nodded her head. "It's been a long day. And tonight is special. I understand." She

reached over and switched on a small table lamp next to her chair. "Come here, child," she urged, as she opened a picture album which lay in her lap. She made room for the girl next to her on the oversized chair.

Eagerly, Julianna came and sat next to her grandmother. She loved the smell of her skin. It was like a mixture of cedar and roses. She snuggled close as the woman reached down and lightly kissed her forehead, then touched a small tear which had begun to course down her dimpled cheek.

Julianna quickly wiped the tear away and squeezed her grandmother's hand. "I'm not really crying, Gramma," she said.

"Well, if you were crying, I wouldn't think it was any of my business unless, of course, you wished to talk about it." She shrugged. "Perhaps it was merely a twinkling star falling from your eye," she offered.

Julianna looked into her grandmother's face as if she knew she was being led into something. "A twinkling star?" she questioned.

"Oh, yes," the woman continued. "You see, it is a well-known fact among us older folks that some children, like you and your brother and sister, possess the beauty of the stars. We see them sparkle in your eyes when you're happy, and then sometimes when you cry, we see them spill out. It makes us sad until we remember something." She turned a page in the picture album and waited for her granddaughter to speak.

Julianna looked at the familiar black and white

photographs for a few moments, then asked, "Until you remember what, Gramma?"

A knowing smile formed on the woman's lips. "That each little star is a miracle, and for every one you lose, you gain another."

"But where do they go?"

"Well, they either evaporate or get wiped away. But they always reappear shining brightly in the heavens and waiting to be plucked again by some believing soul."

Julianna thought for a while, then asked, "So there are miracles in us?"

"In us and all around us, Julianna. But you must believe."

"But how do you know when you've seen a miracle?"

"You'll just know."

A troubled expression came over the child's face. "Billy Grisham has been saying things at school. He and some of the other kids said that there isn't a Santa and that angels don't even exist. Billy says it's all a bunch of lies our parents tell us so we'll be good. They said something else, Gramma, but I don't even want to say it because I know it's not so." The girl bit her fingernail and looked at the white porcelain nativity scene which sat among holly and ivy on the mantel.

Julianna's grandmother followed her gaze and knew then the reason for her sleeplessness, for she also had known such troublesome thoughts in her own childhood. Realizing the magnitude of her granddaughter's dilemma, she chose her words carefully. "It's not important what Billy Grisham or the other children think about such things, Julianna. It's only important what you feel in your own heart. I believe in Santa, because the thought of his existence makes me happy, and he symbolizes the spirit of giving. If that is in my heart, what do I care that others may doubt?" She pointed at the nativity scene and said, "I pray to the spirit of that child and have heard the scoffing of doubters all my life. It doesn't matter because what I feel is deep inside me and they can't touch it." She turned another page in her album and looked at the faded photographs taken so long ago. Then she closed the picture album and pulled out from under it a worn leather-bound book which she placed in the girl's hand.

Julianna opened it and saw that it was written in longhand. Its lines and margins seemed perfect. A title was written at the top of the first page, and, underneath it, a name she knew. The girl looked at her grandmother in surprise.

The woman tapped her finger on the book, then put her hand to her lips and swallowed. "I know a little something about angels, too, Julianna." For a few moments she seemed lost in her thoughts.

"Have you seen them, Gramma? Have you seen angels?"

The woman looked at her granddaughter and then back at the book. She touched it lightly, and the memories it evoked within her began to appear in colorful images. "You wish to know about miracles and

8

angels, Julianna, so I'll give you a story. It's a story I wrote. Read it and perhaps it will answer your questions." With that, she got up from the chair and touched the girl's head with her hand. "Goodnight, dear," she said.

"Goodnight, Gramma."

Julianna watched her grandmother leave the room, then made herself comfortable in the warmth of the chair. And soon she was engrossed in a story written long ago....

The Angel Carver

(January, 1940)

The knock on the front door came just as Tom Spinner placed the last oak log in the fireplace. He brushed his hands against his woolen trousers and looked at his wife, who sat in an armchair as she nursed their infant son in the warm glow of the fire.

"Who could that be, Tom?" she asked while pulling a worn afghan over her shoulder.

Tom looked at the clock above the mantel. It was 6:18 p.m. He glanced out the front window on his way out of the room. "I don't know, honey," he answered. "But I think it's snowing out there."

Rita looked beyond the window pane into the darkness. "The radio was calling for it." She turned her head and looked down at her baby. "There now, sweetheart," she said softly as she tucked the afghan around his body. "Did you hear your daddy? It might be snowing again." She smiled and touched the baby's cheek.

Tom switched on the light in the entrance hall and moved to the front door. A dog was barking outside, and he heard the downshift of Paul Tanner's flatbed Ford a hundred yards down the road in front of his house. As Tom flipped on the porch light and pulled open the door, the wind kicked up and dusted his face with fine snow. He wiped his face and stepped onto the porch. He looked to his right and left, but there was no one there. Tom walked out to the end of the porch and looked down the road at the Tanner place. The house lights were on, and he saw Paul's truck's headlights go out in his driveway. Across the road the river rushed along its rocky banks, and up the road the dog continued its barking. Tom looked down at his front steps and saw faint footprints. He followed them with his eyes, a job made easy by the dusting of snow on the wide-boarded porch. They came and went, and where they had paused at the left side of the front door, there was a package. Tom looked into the darkness and called, "Hello, anybody out there?" But he didn't expect an answer. He stooped and picked up the package, then kicked the snow off his shoes and stepped inside the house.

Rita heard the door shut and looked toward the hallway. "Tom, who is it?"

Tom looked at the package for a moment without answering his wife. It was oddly shaped and about ten inches in length. The wrapping was a coarse brown paper that resembled a grocery bag. Its ends and corners were neatly folded and tucked, and there was a thick string binding around it. Tom turned the package over in his hands and shook it.

"Tom?" Rita's voice sounded worried.

He switched off the hall light and walked into the room. "I'm sorry, honey. Whoever it was is gone, but look," he held out the package.

Rita looked curiously at the strangely shaped parcel. "What is it?" she asked.

"I have no idea." Tom reached into his pants pocket and pulled out a small, horn-handled jack-knife. He unfolded the blade and slipped its razor edge beneath the package bindings. As the string fell to the floor, he was aware of his wife's eager anticipation. Tom turned the package over and examined it more closely. "Look how perfectly this thing is wrapped," he marveled with a curious grin. "I almost hate to undo it."

Rita's curiosity was aroused. She strained her eyes and pointed. "Is that writing there?"

Tom looked more closely at the paper and found a penciled note. "Yes," he answered. "It reads: 'A gift for Zachary.'" The letters were thick and gray. The writer had been careful not to pierce the paper. Tom gently unwrapped the gift and held it up for his wife to see.

Rita was awestruck. She put her hand to her lips.

"Oh, goodness, Tom. It is so beautiful!" She reached out and touched it with her fingers.

Tom shook his head in disbelief. "I've never seen such detail in a carving." He rubbed his thumb along the curved edge of a wing. It was smooth and long. "Look how the grain of the wood lends itself to the contours of the body," he observed. "Look at the placement of the wings. It's as if it could lift right out of my hands." He carefully handed it to his wife.

Rita took it and realized her baby had stopped nursing. "Look, Zack," she whispered. "Look at what *he* brought you."

For an instant the child's eyes opened wide and his small body quivered. Rita cuddled him and kissed his forehead.

Tom moved closer to his wife and son. "Did you see that little twinkle in his eye?"

The baby flailed his arms excitedly and grasped the small outstretched hand of the carving.

"Look," smiled his mother. "He's holding its hand!"

They both laughed.

Later that evening, as Rita tucked little Zack in for the night, Tom came into the room and placed the carving on the shelf above his son's crib. "There," he said. "Someone to watch over you while you sleep, little boy." He reached down and kissed Zack's head, then raised up and put his arms around his wife.

Rita turned in his arms and looked up at him. "It really was him, Tom. That man really did come in the night as they said he would." She rested her face against her husband's chest. "I guess I didn't think that he was real," she admitted.

Tom rubbed his wife's shoulder and squeezed her. "Oh, he's real, honey. There're footprints in the snow to prove that. Tomorrow I'm going to ask Paul Tanner a few questions about him. I'm wondering what he knows."

Outside little Zack's window, silence tamed the night except for the sound of the rushing Tye River.

The dogs up the road huddled together for warmth in their rickety shelter behind the Tea Room. And snow dusted the footprints left by a gentle soul....

Paul Tanner opened the door of his truck and stepped down onto a thin blanket of snow. He shut the door behind him and stood looking at the night sky. The clouds were thin and there was a bright moon over them. It wouldn't snow much more this night, he thought. But it was coming. He felt that. He closed his eyes and let the small, cold crystals fall upon his eyelids. The sensation was pleasant.

The light on the side porch came on, and he saw his wife, Edna, standing at the kitchen door, stirring a pot of something. He walked by the door and waved. "Be there in a minute. I'm gonna fetch a bait of wood."

His wife nodded and returned to her cook stove.

Paul pulled his collar up around his neck. He moved to the back yard where cured firewood lay crisscrossed in neatly stacked ricks under the split-shingled roof of a three-sided shed. The Tye River rushed by at the edge of the yard.

The man stopped at the shed and listened. He loved the sound of the river. Its constant rush had lulled him to sleep nearly every night of his life, except for the time he was out of the country. Only God knew how much he'd missed it then. Instead of the sound of the wind and water of the mountains, there had been the prayers and curses of men, cries and screams and gunfire and explosions. That was a long time ago, a time Paul Tanner wished he could forget. But he couldn't, and the louder the river was, the more it suited him, for somehow it masked the sounds in his memory.

Paul cradled several good-sized sticks of split oak in his arms and walked to the kitchen door. He stood there for a moment and raised his eyes toward the dark silhouette of the mountain. Up there lived a man who knew the sounds in his head, the only other soul he had ever talked to about his past, a man he loved like a brother.

A tap on the glass pane of the door got his attention, and Paul responded with a startled look.

The door opened, and the aroma of fried chicken and bread in the oven swept by him. Edna stood in the doorway, wiping her hands on her apron. "You best get in the house a'fore a cold wind settles in your bones, old man," she scolded playfully while stepping to the side.

Paul went into the house and kissed the rotund woman on her warm cheek. "I got an arm full and a stomach empty, woman. Feed me or knock me in the head."

Edna Tanner closed the door behind her husband and followed him into the front room, where she watched him place the wood in a copper tub by the stove. "Get yourself cleaned up and come on to the table. Biscuits and gravy's just 'bout ready." The woman turned and walked back into the kitchen.

Paul removed his coat and hung it on a rack on the wall in the breezeway. "I'm on my way, Ed," he called. The heat in the house was almost stifling. Paul unfastened the top button of his shirt and rolled his flannel sleeves to his elbows. He came into the kitchen and washed his hands at the spigot. Then he took his chair at the table. Edna brought a basket of fresh biscuits and sat down. The couple bowed their heads.

"Heavenly Father, we thank You for this food. Bless it to the nourishment of our bodies. Bless our loved ones and forgive us our sins. In Christ's name we pray. Amen."

Edna repeated her husband's "amen," and they commenced filling their plates with portions of steaming food.

"Smells mighty good, Ed." Paul mashed his potatoes with his fork to resemble a volcano, then filled the crater with a generous helping of chicken gravy.

Edna poured her husband a glass of milk, laid a fried chicken breast on his plate, and watched him smother it in gravy. "Don't salt nothin', Paul," she said. "Ever'thing's been seasoned enough. 'Sides you don't want your fingers swellin' from too much salt."

"Somethin's comin', Ed." Paul buttered a hot biscuit and reached for the blackberry jam. He smeared a thick portion on half of his biscuit and took a bite.

Edna broke a chicken wing and picked the meat from its bones. "I seen a little snow fallin'," she answered. "It's about as fine as salt, I reckon."

Paul looked out the kitchen window into the blackness. "Charley Druen was down at the Tea Room today and said he'd been by Myrtle Ward's place up on the Piney River yesterday to check on her, and she told him a snow was comin'."

"How's Ma Ward doin'? Did Charley say?" Edna wiped the grease from her fingers with a napkin and bit into a fluffy golden-brown biscuit.

"Said she's doin' all right. Missin' Ned since he went under, but the children check on her enough, I reckon." Paul cleared his throat. "Anyways, you've heard 'bout Ma's gift for callin' the weather."

"What'd she say?"

"Well, she says to Charley that he best get his corn to the mill quick 'cause a blizzard's comin' like we ain't seen a'fore."

Edna took a sip of tea and looked at her husband. "You reckon she's right?"

Paul leaned back in his chair and put both hands on the table. "Some snow's been lingerin' on the ground for weeks now, Ed, like it's waitin' for company. And I got a feelin' company's comin'. Ma Ward's got a knack for calling things."

Edna turned her head and looked out the window toward Priest Mountain. Paul was right about the lingering snow, she thought. The little bit that had fallen three weeks ago hadn't melted much. Instead, it cloaked the mountains like a ragged white coat. It was beautiful in a way, yet ominous.

"Maybe you best git up the holler tomorrow and tell Rachael to come down here and stay a while. I don't much like the idea of her and Maddie gettin' caught up there."

Paul nodded his head. "I'll go up and try to talk 'em down, but you know that daughter of yours is 'bout as stubborn as can be. Thinks that little house up there's the only place she can paint her pictures."

"I know how she is 'bout it, and I can understand it, what with it bein' built by her and Michael." Edna's voice was filled with concern. "But she's got to know, Paul, that Michael wouldn't want her to stay up there and shut folks off like she's done for so long. It ain't good for her, and little Maddie needs to be 'round people more than she is, too. Grievin' the loss of somebody's a hard thing. But somewheres along the line you got to shore up and git on with your life." The woman shook her head sadly. "They ain't got nobody up there 'cept for Beecher Whitman, and he's blind. Shoot, if somethin' was to happen up there, they don't even have a telephone."

Paul thumped his fingers on the worn oak table.

"Well, Ed, Beecher's been up there a long time, and he can get around the hollers and ridge tops better than most men I know with two good eyes. You know, Rachael's always been crazy 'bout him. And Maddie, well, that little girl loves him 'bout as much as she would her own daddy. They look out for one another up there."

Edna shook her head and sighed. "Look out for one 'nother?" she questioned in exasperation. "Paul, Beecher Whitman's blind. He can't look out for nobody!"

Paul felt a twinge of anger. He rubbed his face with his hand and looked away from his wife. He began to perspire. His mind raced back, and suddenly he was on a churned-up battlefield in France. There were explosions all around him and flares which lit up the smoke-filled sky and a ground drenched in blood and littered with torn and mangled bodies. His mind's eye recaptured the unforgettable silhouettes of bullet-riddled soldiers, tangled in barbed wire, their lifeless bodies frozen like grotesque scarecrows in a burned-out cornfield. He heard the call of his comrades to charge and remembered the feel and the sound of the mud sucking at his boots as he came up out of the trench and rushed toward the enemy.

Guns fired, bombs exploded, and lead and metal ripped through men all around him. But Paul Tanner had continued onward, his fear choked by adrenaline and a will to survive. He rushed forward, firing his weapon and screaming, until hot lead pierced his chest and leg and he fell to the ground, helpless. At first, there was no pain. The movements around him seemed as if in slow motion. Screams were echoed. A fallen soldier, practically cut in half by enemy fire, lay crying in agony for his mother. Paul looked beyond the smoke of the battlefield and wondered how the stars could dangle so beautifully above the foolishness of men. He watched the heavens through the smoke until a face replaced the stars and strong hands lifted him up.

"Come on, Paul. I'm going to carry you out of here," a voice spoke.

Paul was slung over the massive shoulder of a man and carried back toward the trench. More bombs burst and shrapnel tore through the clothes and the skin of his bearer, but on he went, determined to save this one man, this friend from his childhood.

Later, as Paul Tanner lay on a stretcher in the safety of a trench, he could not recognize the bloodied face of the man who had carried him to safety. But he knew the voice well. He had always known the voice.

"Paul?" Edna Tanner shook the arm of her husband.

He seemed startled.

"I'm sorry, honey," she apologized. "I know that Beecher means a lot to you. You know I'm grateful to him beyond words."

Paul turned and patted her hand. He nodded, but didn't speak. He knew she didn't mean to be cruel. She had always thought a lot of Beecher Whitman. She was just concerned about Rachael and Maddie, that was all.

"I'll make a run up Silver Creek tomorrow, Ed." Paul squeezed his wife's hand. "Don't you worry, now."

Later that night, Paul Tanner stepped out on his porch and looked at the mountain. The snow had stopped, but the thin clouds he had watched earlier in the evening were now thickening. "Old Ma Ward is right," he said aloud. "Somethin' is comin'...."

Rachael Lundy bit her lip and squinted her dark eyes. "I'm going to give it one more try, Maddie," she said with determination. "Now, hold on!"

The little girl grasped the edge of her seat and mimicked the facial expression of her mother. "Hit it, Mama!" she called out.

With that, Rachael touched the gas pedal and eased off the clutch. She heard the sound of tires spinning on ice and felt the Ford slowly begin to move forward. "Come on, baby," she coaxed.

Maddie repeated the words of her mother. "Come on, baby," she urged.

The Ford crept up the incline inch by inch, until the rear wheels touched the grit of the dirt road. Suddenly, the vehicle lunged forward. Rachael quickly took her foot off the gas pedal and hit the brake and clutch right in the nick of time. The car swerved on the narrow mountain road and stopped dangerously close to the edge.

Maddie looked out her window and down the mountainside. "It's a long way down there," she cautioned.

Her mother uttered a sigh of relief. She leaned over and looked out the passenger window. The drop was not straight down, but certainly impressive in its descent. The slope was densely populated by hemlock, oak, and maple trees.

Rachael tapped her daughter on the knee. "Let's make a note not to ever go over the edge here, Maddie. If the trees don't stop you, you'll end up way down there in the creek."

Maddie grabbed her mother's hand and shook it. "It's a deal, Mama!" she said. She turned and looked down the mountainside, past the trees and saw the splashing white water of Silver Creek. She shuddered to think how cold it was. "Let's go, Mama. I told Beecher we'd come to see him today."

Rachael put the car in first gear and turned the wheels back onto the road. "I know, honey. I've got to get him a bag of flour, too."

"He makes the best biscuits, Mama. How does he make biscuits so good?" Maddie paused and thought about what she had said, then added, "Not that yours aren't good, Mama. It's just that his have a little more fluff to them than yours do, and when I bite into one, it's almost like I'm a giant biting into a white, fluffy cloud."

Rachael saw that her daughter was playing with a strand of blue yarn. The girl was trying to form a design of some sort by sticking various ones of her fingers in and around loops and tightening the strand. Nothing seemed to work and finally the child dropped the yarn in her lap and crossed her arms over her chest. "Anyway," she continued, "sometimes Beecher will get out the honey, and I just love it then because we have honey biscuits and tea. He says a proper lady never slurps her tea, and sometimes, if I make a little noise, he acts like it hurts his ears. He's funny."

Rachael smiled, and Maddie saw it.

"What are you smiling for, Mama?"

Rachael slowed the Ford for a blind curve and answered, "Well, Beecher wins you over with honey biscuits. He's done it with you, and he did it with me when I was young."

Maddie thought for a minute. "Well, I wouldn't care if he couldn't make cornbread. I'd still love him."

"I know you would, Maddie. I would, too. He's a special man."

Fifteen minutes later Rachael Lundy pulled the Ford into the rough parking lot of the Tea Room.

The Tea Room was the closest thing to a general store that the folks around Tyro, Virginia, had in 1940. It had once been a schoolhouse. It got its name from a group of ladies who congregated once a week for quilting bees during the '30's. As they quilted and discussed the latest happenings in the mountain community, they'd have tea and cookies. After a while,

word got around that there was a little more than just tea being served at their weekly gathering. At first there were only whispers, but when their fondness for mountain brew became common knowledge, the local gossips smirked and began referring to their meeting place as the "Tea" Room. Even after the quilting bees came to an end, the name remained.

Its frame structure looked as if it needed a new coat of white paint. Its red tin roof was rusted. There was a boarded porch out front, protected from the sun and rain by a low tin roof. Assorted cane chairs, some four-legged, some rocking, were lined up against the wall at the rear of the porch, which served as a gathering place. When the weather was cold, the chairs were moved inside. The interior of the store was not unlike other general stores of the day. A red Coca-Cola chest-type cooler filled with sodas sat along one wall. Sometimes when Jim Gresby, the one-armed owner of the Tea Room, was outside, children would stick their hands into the icy water just to see how long they could stand it.

The board and batten walls to the sides and rear of the store contained shelves from the floor to the ceiling. Almost anything one wanted, from nails to piece goods, flour to toys, mousetraps to sugar, could be found on these. Livestock and poultry feeds in bags were located in a small storeroom at the rear. But what made the Tea Room unique was the pool table which stood in the center of the store. A low, wide-bladed ceiling fan hovered about four feet above the center of the pool table. The fan was usually on.

Saturday night was pool night at the Tea Room, but there was almost always some sort of activity going on around the table, even if it was just a couple of old men trading stories.

Lemus Boford, who was thought to be in his mid-nineties, had a regular chair near the front corner of the table right next to the wood stove; and Billy Gump kept a wooden fold-out chair at the end of the table away from the wood stove. Billy lived in a shack along Harper's Creek west of Tyro and didn't come out of his hollow often. This was just fine with most folks because he was known to be rather spare with a cake of soap. Jim Gresby politely discouraged Billy from coming by in the winter, preferring rather that the "old goat" visit during fair weather. In the outdoors he was more tolerable to one's sense of smell. It was always interesting to see old men checking the wind direction before choosing a chair when Billy Gump was present.

The Tea Room was quite an establishment, and many who frequented it were certainly characters.

Rachael Lundy knew them all.

Jim Gresby was leaning on the edge of the counter near the big cash register and reading the newspaper when Rachael came into the store, followed by Maddie.

"Well, hello, ladies," said the big man, with a smile.

Rachael smiled back. "Hi, Jim."

Maddie acted coy, making sure Jim saw her eyeing the candy jar.

Jim stepped to the other side of the cash register where the little girl stood gazing into the jar. He took the lid off the jar and said, "Go ahead, Maddie. It's on the house."

Maddie began to reach into the jar, then looked over at her mother.

Rachael smiled and held up one finger. Maddie's eyes got big, and she reached into the jar and brought out a fat peppermint stick. She broke off a piece and slipped the remainder into her coat pocket. Before she popped the candy into her mouth, she thanked the man for his kindness.

Jim Gresby had never had children of his own, but he was fond of them, and all the children around Tyro knew him to be a big old softy. He reached under the counter, and Maddie heard him drop several pieces of something into a paper bag. She stood on her tiptoes to see what he was up to.

When he raised up, Jim handed the bag to the girl. "Now, Miss Maddie, here's a little horehound candy for you."

Maddie took the bag. "Oh, thank you, Jim."

Jim smiled and winked at her mother. "Rachael, if there's anything I can help you with, just let me know."

"Thank you, Jim. We don't need much today."

Maddie busied herself at the counter with the toy section of the Sears-Roebuck catalog while her mother located two five-pound bags of flour.

"Your daddy come by a little while ago, Rachael," Jim announced. "Said he was headin' up the holler to see y'all and to visit Beecher later on today."

"Oh?" Rachael looked up. "We're going to drop by the house. We'll probably see him there."

The front door of the store opened, and a little bell at the rear of the room sounded. "Hi, Jim." It was Tom Spinner. He looked around the room. Maddie looked up at the young man and smiled.

"Hello, young lady." Tom nodded his head.

Jim spoke up, "Tom, do you know Maddie?"

"Don't believe I've had the pleasure, Jim."

"Well, that's Maddie and her mama, Rachael Lundy."

Rachael approached the counter and set the two bags of flour and her other purchases in front of Jim. She reached out her hand. "It's so nice to meet you, Mr. Spinner."

"Tom, please," responded the surprised man. "How did you know my last name?"

"My father is Paul Tanner, and he has spoken very highly of you."

Tom smiled and nodded his head. "So you are Paul and Edna's daughter. My wife, Rita, and I own two of your paintings." Tom put his fingers to his temple. "*The Trout Pool* and *Winter Woods*. We love your work. Bought them at a store in Lynchburg. Shelby's, I think."

"Yes, Shelby's sells a lot of my paintings. I'm glad you like my work. Thank you."

"When we realized that Paul and Edna were your parents, we were just flabbergasted!" He laughed. "They came by the house after we moved here, and

Edna just casually mentioned that the paintings on our wall were done by their daughter. Well, you can imagine our surprise and delight, for we thought maybe we'd get to meet you sometime."

Rachael smiled.

Maddie spoke up, "Do you and your wife have any children, Mr. Spinner?"

"Why, yes, Maddie. We have a little boy named Zack. He's six weeks old."

Maddie was excited. "Oh, good!" she exclaimed. "Mama, can we go see their baby? Please?" Maddie hunched her shoulders and clasped her hands tightly.

"Now, Maddie, it's not polite to invite yourself to someone's home." Rachael raised her eyebrow at her daughter, then, embarrassed, smiled at Tom. "Sorry, Tom," she said.

"Oh, no, no. Really, we'd love for you to come over. Rita will be so surprised. She's there with the baby now. Here, let me call down to the house." Tom reached for the phone at the end of the counter. "Jim, do you mind?"

"Oh, no, go ahead." Jim chuckled and began ringing up Rachael's purchases.

Tom was on the phone for half a minute before he put down the receiver and turned to Rachael. "Rita is ecstatic! She just got the baby up from his nap, so now would be a great time if you can stop by."

Rachael looked at her daughter.

Maddie formed the word "Please" on her lips.

"Well, all right, Tom, if you're sure it will be no inconvenience."

The young man shook his head. "It's no inconvenience at all."

Jim Gresby finished ringing up Rachael's order. "That'll be five dollars and forty-five cents, Rachael."

She reached into her purse and counted out six dollars.

Jim gave her back change. "You must be expecting company, what with all that flour."

Rachael laughed. "Oh, mercy, no, Jim. One bag is for Beecher."

Tom was looking at merchandise on the shelves behind Jim and, in particular, at a vacant area on a shelf near the front window. His curiosity was aroused when he heard the name.

Jim shook open a paper bag and set it on the counter top where he began filling it with Rachael's purchases. "How is Beecher doin', Rachael? I ain't seen him for a spell, and we done run plum out of his carvings. They go like hot cakes, once word gets 'round that I've got a new batch of 'em. Tom, here, bought up the last two. I swear Beech ought to get 'em into some of them fancy city stores. He could make all kinds of money."

While Jim talked, he opened the cash register and reached to the back of the tray for an envelope with Beecher Whitman's name on it and handed it to Rachael. "Here, Rachael, give this to Beecher and tell him to get more carvings to me when he can. I can sell 'em fast as he can whittle 'em."

Rachael took the envelope and put it in her purse. "I'll pass the word along, Jim. I'm sure he'll send some more carvings by Dad or me soon. And by the way, he's doing real good. But you know Beecher. He's not going to come off the mountain without a good reason."

Jim shook his head. "I know that for sure, Rachael, but the Lord don't make 'em better than Beecher. He just don't."

"Beecher's got lots of carvings, Mr. Gresby. His house is full of them. Even the posts that hold up his porch roof have faces carved all over them. And he has all of these beautiful wind chimes hanging on his porch." Maddie was almost breathless when her mother put her hand on her shoulder and guided her to the door behind Tom Spinner.

Rachael looked back at the store owner. "He won her over a long time ago, Jim." ·

The man waved his hand. "You tell him I said howdy."

"I will," answered Rachael, as she stepped outside.

The door closed, and Jim Gresby turned up the radio. He just missed the weather forecast. A song by Bing Crosby was playing. Jim looked out the window at Priest Mountain. The sky was dark and still. Perhaps Ma Ward was right, he thought. Charley Druen believed her, and Paul Tanner had seemed real concerned about what she had said. So much so that he was considering talking to Rachael about her and Maddie spending a few days with him and Edna. The forecast had called for snow, but they didn't always get it right. Maybe this one, if it came, was going to be different. Maybe this one was really going to be something....

Beecher Whitman leaned forward, his strong hands gripping the cedar rail of his front porch. He could hear Silver Creek as it rushed down the hollow. The man smelled the air. It was cold and moist. The scent of wood smoke from his chimney lay heavy in his nostrils. That was a sign to him. The smoke was laying low. Snow was on the way, for sure, he thought. It was too cold for rain. He could've depended on the radio for the weather forecast, but he preferred instead to feel the air and listen to the sounds around him. The squirrels and chipmunks had been busier than usual, and deer were feeding on acorns right up to his front porch during the night. They all seemed ravenous. Nature, as always, told of impending weather, and Beecher liked to listen to it, although most men had forgotten how. He was a rare individual.

Beecher Whitman had been born and raised in the shadow of Priest Mountain and the hollow that bore his name. His father, Isaac, had brought his wife, Ellen, to the mountain in the spring of 1880. No one knew where they had come from or what work Isaac had done in the past, but there was money in the family and the Whitmans used it to purchase 300 acres of heavily forested mountainside. Isaac had no interest in farming and only cleared enough land for a fine cedar-log cabin, which he and Ellen built, and a good-sized garden. In the beginning, he'd cut firewood and sell it around Tyro and Massie's Mill, for there was a good amount of dead timber on his land and he wanted to take some out. He was careful to leave some of the dead wood for birds and critters that were dependent on it. One local woodcutter had made the statement that Isaac Whitman had a fortune in hardwood if he ever decided to sell. But the Whitmans had no intention of selling.

The forest was what Isaac had always longed for after a life in the city, with its crime and stench and breakneck speed. He needed it for his soul. Ellen needed it for her health. They chose a place for their cabin in a secluded hollow along Silver Creek, and there, among giant hemlocks, oaks, and maples, they carved out the second part of their lives. Behind the cabin, Priest Mountain rose like a huge bear turned on its side. Its girth and height and long finger ridges protected their home from the harsh winter winds that blew through the mountain hollows. Sometimes when a snow would come and lie like a thick white blanket over the mountains, Isaac would stand at his front door and call his wife to come see. "Look," he would say, "It's as if the forest and we have risen into the clouds."

Ellen would move into the warm embrace of her husband and spin silent, wistful thoughts. She'd feel the strength in his arms and look upon the rugged handsomeness of his face and wish for the one thing they had not been able to share. Time was carrying her youthfulness away, and they both knew her child-bearing years would soon be behind her. Seldom did they talk openly about it, but it was constantly on both their minds.

Time had passed and wishes faded until the last wisp of hope lay in the prayers of these two good-hearted people. Now, had their prayers been of selfish origin, they might have realized nothing in return unless it was by chance. But one night as they prayed, it was as if their spirits were one. That was when the angels heard. That was when messages were sent into the spirit world like ripples on a still pond.

Months later a child was born into the home of Isaac and Ellen Whitman. It was a son, and they named him Beecher.

During his childhood Beecher brought much happiness into the lives of his parents. Ellen doted on her little man and nurtured his confidence whenever possible. When at the age of five he proudly brought her his first creel of trout for the supper table, he was not only lauded as a good fisherman, but as the finest fisherman in the mountains. Ellen figured her husband had caught some of the fish, but Isaac assured her he had lain beneath a shady maple tree the whole time the boy fished and had slept peacefully.

Quite by accident Isaac Whitman began preaching

in a little stone church beside the Tye River while Beecher was a youngster. The Whitmans had attended Harmony Church regularly, and one Sunday after the long-time pastor, Reverend John Runyon, passed away and before the congregation was able to locate a new preacher, Isaac got up in the pulpit and delivered an outstanding sermon without notes or even a Bible in his hand. He was commissioned on the spot, for very little pay, and accepted his task with a jovial heart. From that time on, he was known as Preacher Whitman.

It was during a Sunday gathering on a spring day when Beecher was only seven that he overheard some church women talking quietly about someone who was too old to carry a child. He wondered who it might be, as the old women seemed concerned. Later he learned that the one they had talked about was his own mother.

"Will you be all right, Mama?" he had asked her one night.

Ellen put her arm around her son's shoulder and brought him closer to her. She spoke softly and told him what he wanted to hear. "I'll be fine, son. Don't you worry."

But Beecher was worried, and the glow from the fireplace glistened in the wells of his tears.

Soon after that night, Beecher was sent in haste down the mountain for young Dr. Spangler, but when they arrived back at the cabin, the baby had been born. Beecher watched as his mother slept, and he was allowed to hold the baby girl for a while until the doctor took her and placed her on the bed beside her mother.

"Something's not right, Isaac." Dr. Spangler's voice was low as he raised up from the newborn after examining her. "Her breathing is labored and her heartbeat is irregular."

Isaac Whitman put his hand on his son's shoulder and guided him toward his room. "It's time to go to bed, son," he said with a grave voice.

Beecher pulled away and ran back to his mother's bedside. He reached over and kissed her and then touched the baby's cheek with trembling lips. "I'll pray for you, little sister," he cried. "Don't you worry none. Beecher's got somethin' pretty for you. Somethin' to watch over you."

Isaac heard his son's words and fought back the tears in his eyes, wiping his face with his hand as he looked at the doctor.

Then the boy whispered in his sister's tiny ear, "I'll bring it to you later. You just sleep with Mama now." He kissed the baby, then turned and hugged his father. He left the two men with mother and child.

For hours after that, the boy sat in his room and carved on a piece of wood with a jackknife his father had given him. He had never before done more than whittle on a stick, but that night was different. He had made a promise, and he carved the image of a recurring dream. And the image was an angel.

That was a long time ago. Some memories are like well-worn paths we walk alone and often. Such was this memory for Beecher Whitman as he turned slowly from his place on the porch and stepped into his cabin. He did not stumble or feel his way along as he passed through the spacious room. He knew it as one knows one's own face. He walked straight to the wood bin located next to the back door and lifted two good-sized split logs into his arms, then walked to the center of the room where the wood stove stood and placed them neatly upon the embers. He closed the heavy iron stove door and walked around a wide-armed rocking chair to a table which stood against the wall at the rear of the house. The table was of solid oak, and its surface was square. Beecher sat down on a sturdy oak chair and picked up a carving knife with a short blade....

Maddie Lundy cradled her arms and acccpted the baby. "He is just so beautiful," she declared, as she played with his tiny fingers. Zack grasped her thumb and squeezed it.

"Oh, my!" she said. "You're a strong little thing. I want to take him home, Mama," she proclaimed.

Rachael laughed and cleared her throat. "I don't think Mr. And Mrs. Spinner would like that, Maddie."

They all laughed.

Rachael looked around the room. "I love what you've done with the house, Rita." She walked over to the mantel and studied the clock. "I see you have a passion for antiques."

Rita nodded, "Oh, goodness, yes. If it weren't for old things, we wouldn't have much. Tom's parents moved to Florida two years ago and decided to travel light. He's an only child, so we ended up with a lot of furniture and things. They had a large house in Staunton and wanted to scale down a bit."

The phone rang, and Tom excused himself and walked into the hallway.

"He's looking for a call from New York," Rita confessed eagerly. "Tom's a playwright, and Jonathan Eckley, who produces plays on Broadway, is interested in his latest work."

"Oh, that's wonderful, Rita."

"Well, it will be if he decides to do it. Tom was an English professor at the university in Charlottesville and decided to take a three-year hiatus to devote his time to writing."

Rachael understood. "Sometimes that's what it takes. It's hard to hold a job and pursue your passion."

Rita agreed. "And frustrating, too! Tom felt like he wasn't giving his teaching or his writing a fair chance, so here we are with a stone house in the country and nothing but time on our hands." Rita made a face. "For three years, that is."

"Oh?" questioned Rachael.

"We saved up for this, and our parents helped us

get the house. We've allowed three years for the writing to pay off or it's back to the halls of academia." Rita crossed her fingers for Rachael to see.

"I vote for a place in the country," said Rachael, "and Tom's name in lights. It sounds like you've got a plan and you're going through with it. That's further than most people get. Most people settle for so much less than what they really want. It's inspiring to see someone reach for the stars."

Tom hung up the phone and came back into the room.

Rita looked at him with anticipation. "Well?" she asked.

Tom clapped his hands. "He likes it a lot, but wants to know if I can spice up the third and fourth acts with a little more humor." Tom paused for a moment, then added, "I think I can do that. I told him I'd have something in the mail to him in a week."

Rita rushed forward and gave her husband a big hug and kiss. "All right, honey!"

The young man kissed his wife, then changed the subject. "Rachael, I want you to see something. I'll be right back." With that, he hurried out the room and up the stairs.

In no time, he was back. "Have you ever seen anything like this?" he asked, while offering her the carving that had been left at his door the night before.

Rachael took the carving from him and turned it over in her hands. She looked down at her daughter. "Recognize this, Maddie?"

Maddie's face lit up as she spoke. "Yes, it's one of

Beecher's!" She looked at Tom. "We have two of them. One is Mama's, and one is mine."

Tom Spinner scratched his head. "How long has he been doing this?"

Rachael answered, "Since he was a little boy, before the turn of the century. There are folks around here who have very old ones. It's amazing how good a carver he was even as a child."

"But I'm told he's blind."

"There are varying degrees of blindness, Tom." Rachael felt her face flush. She was aware that she needed to control herself. She felt protective of Beecher.

"But I was told that Beecher Whitman is blind, Rachael," Tom repeated. "That he can't see light at all. And last night there were footprints in the snow on my front porch, and this was left for our baby."

Rita spoke up, "We'd been told about this angel carver, but thought it was just a local legend."

"Don't get us wrong, Rachael," Tom was apologetic. "It's not like we don't appreciate it. It's beautiful. But how can a blind man carve an angel like this or, for that matter, anything. It's unbelievable. And how could he find his way to our front door when he lives half way up a mountain?" Tom Spinner stopped and took a breath. He walked over to a dark mahogany bookshelf in the far corner of the room. "Look at these." He pointed to the carved figures of a bear and an Indian with his hunting bow drawn. "I bought these at the Tea Room this morning. They've got Beecher Whitman's initials carved into their bases. I wanted another angel but—"

Maddie interrupted as she handed little Zack back to his mother. "You don't get an angel unless you have a baby." Then she smiled. "If you want another angel, you and your wife have to have another baby."

Rachael agreed. "Maddie is right, Tom. Beecher doesn't sell the angels. He never has."

"But, why?" Tom was astounded.

Rachael put up her hand and shook her head. "All I can tell you is this, Tom. Beecher is a master woodcarver, and only he and the Lord know his inspiration or even how he does what he does. As far as how he delivers them, it has always been a mystery. No one has ever seen him do it, but whenever a child is born around here, an angel appears."

Tom threw his hands up in resignation. "I just don't understand how it can be," he said. Then he took the angel from Rachael and pointed to its base. "I think it's interesting that his initials are missing from this carving. Look."

Rachael didn't have to look. "The angels are never signed. I guess we all just assume that Beecher carves them."

Tom shook his head. "There're just some things about Beecher Whitman I'll never understand."

Rachael helped Maddie with her coat. "You're right about that, Tom. And you're not the first person ever to say that, either."

They walked to the front door.

"Come to think of it, you won't be the last." Rachael held out her hand, and Tom squeezed it. She looked at Rita and smiled. "Zack is beautiful. You are both blessed."

The Spinners agreed.

Tom opened the door, and Rachael and Maddie stepped out onto the porch. It was still and cold outside. Their breaths hung like thin clouds around their faces. Rita said goodbye and went back into the house.

Tom felt as if he had hit a nerve in questioning Rachael about a man for whom she obviously had strong sentiments. But his curiosity was piqued.

"Rachael, please know that I do not intend to be disrespectful of Mr. Whitman," he explained. "It's just that we are so intrigued by him."

Rachael understood. There had been others who had asked questions about Beecher. And in the little community of Tyro, there was usually someone to answer them. But there was no one who knew more about Beecher Whitman than the Tanners and the Lundys.

Rachael reached for the long flannel scarf that Maddie had wrapped haphazardly around her neck. She tucked it into the child's coat collar so that it protected the lower part of Maddie's face from the cold air. Then she straightened and looked at Tom Spinner. Her voice was gentle. "Tom, Beecher wasn't blind all of his life. He and my father grew up together and became best of friends." She looked down at her daughter and pulled her close to her side. "They still are," she added. "During the war they fought together in France. They were at Belleau Wood and Chateau-

Thierry. They were at the awful battle of the Meuse-Argonne, where so many men lost their lives."

Tom knew of these places. His own father was a doughboy and had been wounded in the First World War. Compassion filled him as he listened.

"It was at Meuse-Argonne that Beecher lost his sight while carrying my father to safety." The young woman tried to smile, but the words she spoke brought tears to her eyes. She wiped them away with her hand and apologized.

Tom put his hand gently on her shoulder. "No, Rachael, I'm sorry. I didn't know. It was just my foolish curiosity. I see why Mr. Whitman is so important to you and your family."

Rachael lifted her head and took a deep breath, "Oh, he is, Tom," she said. "He brought my father back from the war. He risked his own life for the life of another. There is no greater courage. There is no greater gift."

The man smiled. "Thank you, Rachael. I learned something that I won't forget. And it really is all I need to know about your friend."

A few minutes later Rachael pulled her Ford into her parents' driveway. Maddie flung open the car door and ran onto the porch.

Edna Tanner met her at the kitchen door....

Paul Tanner looked down the steep mountainside as his flatbed truck crept up the narrow mountain road. He saw white water in Silver Creek and thought it looked a little above normal for that time of year.

Paul was the owner and sole timber cruiser for Tanner Lumber Company, which was a family operation founded by his father in 1895. His father, Henry, taught his only son everything about the woods, and by the age of thirteen, Paul could walk through a given stretch of timber and identify and age the trees so precisely that his father named him the company's official cruiser, a job Paul loved and dedicated himself to after school and on Saturdays. When he was sixteen, he was made full-time cruiser and partner in the family business. His timber price estimations were always fair, and at a time when there was little concern for conservation among timber cutters, Paul was careful to leave a portion of mature seeding trees to ensure the continuity of a healthy regrowth.

At eighteen, Paul married the youngest daughter of Jacob and Mary Gilliam, who lived up the south fork of the Piney River on the other side of the mountain. Edna was two years older than Paul and wanted to begin a family as soon as possible. Rachael was born within a year of their marriage. She was the couple's only child.

Rachael was a beautiful and talented girl who showed an ability at an early age to sketch the everyday life of the mountain folk around her. She was eight years old in 1917, when her father volunteered for service and became a Marine. In that year, America entered the European war, and for almost two years, Paul Tanner was gone. In his absence, Rachael was frightened and saw the war as a distant monster who crept closer during the night. Her sketches during that period revealed her fears.

Rachael's fears disappeared with the war's end and the return of her father. She began to give her full attention to painting, and when she was still only ten, she sold her first painting at the Tea Room. Her talent became her passion, and her parents helped build her confidence with their love and encouragement.

Upon graduation from high school, she attended college in Staunton, where she fell deeply in love with her art professor, Michael Lundy. They were married in 1928, and five years later Rachael gave birth to a daughter. Their happiness seemed endless, as Michael taught his classes and promoted his young wife's work. Their careers blossomed together until one day three years after the birth of their daughter, Michael died suddenly of a heart attack.

After that, the little house she and Michael had built near Beecher's Hollow for weekend retreats became the permanent home of Rachael and her daughter. That was where she painted and mended her heart and soul. There in the shadow of the mountain she lived her life insulated from a world of sad surprises. Her money came to her in the form of checks from art galleries that sold her paintings. Her weekly outings were to the Tea Room for groceries and to her parents' house. Her parents took Maddie to Harmony Church on Sundays. Rachael did not attend. Instead, she would walk up the winding road and deeper into the hollow to where she found strength in the presence of a man she had known all her life, a man who listened as a kindred spirit.

Paul Tanner rounded the blind curve in the road and stopped the truck. He looked down at the edge of the road and saw where car tires had skidded to a halt. There was ice on the road. A grove of tall, thick hemlocks kept the sun from warming the ground there and what little ice had melted during the day had frozen during the night. It was a very dangerous place. He let out the clutch and eased around the turn until he came to a rough driveway that led up the hill to his daughter's house. He stopped and looked up the hill. The car was gone, so he continued on the main road. He looked at his watch. It was close to noon. Beecher would have some tea on. Besides, he had a rick of wood on the bed of his truck for his friend. He drove up the mountain, crested a finger ridge, then turned down into Beecher's Hollow....

The teapot began to whistle, and the man laid down his carving knife and rose from his work table. The vision of his dream was almost completed. He covered it with a cloth and set it aside. Then he walked over to the wood stove and reached up, unhooking two heavy clay cups which hung by their handles from a beam. He moved to a shelf along the rear wall of the house and pried the lid off the second tin container, reached in and took out two tea bags he had filled and tied. He reached to his left and counted three jars over for the one which contained some honey.

When Paul Tanner walked up on the front porch, he saw his friend at the door. The door swung open and a hand reached out to him. He took it in a firm grip.

"Howdy, Beecher," he said, entering the cabin. The aroma of the house was an unmistakable combination of rich pipe tobacco and the split pine with which he started his fires. The small table where Beecher did most of his carvings was cleared of debris and displayed two steaming cups and a jar of honey. A basket of biscuits covered with a cloth had been placed in the middle of the table. "I reckon you must've heard me when I turned off the main road," Paul commented while taking off his jacket.

Beecher opened the stove door and laid two oak logs on the glowing embers. He closed the door and walked to the table. "Have something with me, Paul." He motioned for his company to sit down, and he took a chair. "Tea and biscuits with honey. Remember?" He smiled.

As Paul sat down, he looked at the man before him and noticed the broad shoulders and the straight back. Beecher's muscles bulged beneath his flannel shirt, and his hands were strong and calloused. His legs were long, yet stout. Beecher Whitman was a man of the mountains. A man who had refused to let fate rule him.

"I remember," Paul answered with a grin. "You got your mama's talent for biscuits, Beecher." Paul reached into the basket and lifted one out. It was light brown and hot. He pulled it apart and bit into the steaming fluff. "Um, Beecher, don't you ever tell Edna how to fix 'em like this or I'll get fat as a hog." He unscrewed the top on the honey jar and filled a teaspoon with the thick, golden nectar. He dabbed a little on the remainder of his biscuit and stirred the rest into his tea.

Beecher chuckled. "Didn't expect you up here 'til tomorrow, Paul. You lookin' for the girls or just want to drop off that wood on your truck?" Beecher spread some honey on his biscuit and nibbled at it.

"How'd you know I had wood for you?"

Beecher touched his nose with his finger. "I smelled it when you came in," he answered.

Paul figured as much. The man's senses were keen

beyond reason. He'd read once that some folks who lacked certain senses excelled in others, and he didn't doubt it. Beecher's hearing was also acute, and his sense of direction, superb. Unhurried, he could walk through the forest for miles and come back to the same spot that he started from without bumping into the first tree or falling off a cliff. "It has to do with sound and feel," he had once told Paul. But he never really explained it beyond that. If he was in a hurry, he'd carry a stick to warn him of obstacles. But Beecher didn't hurry much. He just moved about from one thing to another in a steady, but relaxed, manner. He didn't lack for anything. The big one-story cabin was fully and comfortably furnished. Paul or Rachael brought his groceries every other week from the Tea Room. Paul kept him fully supplied with winter firewood.

"Well, I thought I'd best come up and offer a room in the house for Rachael and Maddie. Ma Ward says a blizzard's comin' like we ain't seen a'fore." Paul sipped his tea and looked around the house. Everything was neat and clean. The wood bin was full. "You look like you might be expecting a little weather yourself, Beecher."

Beecher offered another biscuit to his friend.

Paul declined, and his host pushed the basket to the side.

"I reckon somethin's comin', Paul." He hunched his wide shoulders and leaned forward on his elbows, resting his chin on his hands. "Animals have been storing up and feeding night and day around the house. Squirrels are too busy to chatter much, and there seems a quietness comin' over the mountain." Beecher took a gulp of tea and added, "Myrtle's probably right. It wouldn't be a bad idea for the girls to go down with you and Edna, but I wouldn't get my hopes up. You know your daughter."

"Well, what about you, Beecher?" Paul asked. "You know you're welcome to come on down 'til things get over with." Paul knew the answer before he asked the question.

Beecher turned his face toward the window. "Thanks, Paul, but weather hasn't ever run me out of this hollow." He played his knuckles on the table a few times. "Thanks anyway, though. You tell Edna I said that."

Paul shook his head and looked at his friend. He was square of jaw, and his cheekbones were set high. His mouth was dignified, and the only wrinkles in his fair, clean skin were smile creases that began just below and to the sides of his nostrils and coursed down like half moons toward either side of his chin. There were some scars around his eyes, and when in the presence of others, he wore a pair of rounded dark glasses. His hair was brown and neatly combed. There were flecks of grey in his sideburns and at his temples. Most folks would have called Beecher Whitman a handsome fellow, even dignified.

"I'll tell her, Beecher, but you know she'll just shake her head and call you an old fool under her breath, even though she doesn't mean it."

Beecher smiled and nodded.

Paul looked around the room again, but didn't talk.

Beecher felt his awkwardness. "Is somethin' wrong, Paul?" he asked.

Paul turned in his seat and looked into the face of his boyhood friend. "They were talking at the Tea Room the other day 'bout what's goin' on in Europe. You know, Beecher, them Germans are invadin' the countries around 'em. They took Poland in September, and a couple days later, France and Britain declared war on Germany." Paul swallowed and rubbed his chin. "I don't know, Beecher; it's like the devil's blowin' fire into the hearts of men. It's like what we done a few years back was for nothin'. Now, it's comin' back."

Beecher thought for a minute before speaking. "Paul, what we did years ago did some folks some good then. But war don't settle much in the long run. It's just a way of punishin' bullies on a big scale, then drawin' up new lines for them to step over the next time. It looks to me like war and peace are a perpetual thing. You're born into either one or the other, and if you live long enough, you see it all."

There was a long moment of silence before Paul said what was in his heart. "It all came back to me lately, Beecher, and I just want you to know again that I'm thankful for what you done for me back then. You didn't have to do that."

Beecher drank the remainder of his tea and set the cup down on the table.

"Yes, I did, Paul," he answered without a quiver

in his voice. "You're like a brother to me, and I'd do it again." He felt a crumb on the surface of the table, picked it up and popped it into his mouth. "Only, I'd run you back to the trench a different way."

Paul reached across the table and gripped Beecher's hand. He squeezed it for a second, then got up from his chair. He wiped his moistened eyes with his shirt sleeve and slipped on his jacket. "Where do you want that wood stacked, Beecher?" he asked on his way to the front door.

Beecher was right behind him with coat and hat in hand. "We'll stack it up on the front porch, Paul. Then if Myrtle's storm comes, it'll be in easy reach."

The two men walked out the door, and Beecher closed it behind them.

Twenty minutes later, he said goodbye to his life-long friend and heard him drive away. He raised his face and inhaled the cold air. He listened to the splash and gurgle of Silver Creek, then turned his ears beyond it to the silence of the mountain. He walked back into his cabin, thinking he'd have a talk with Rachael later on. It would probably be a good idea for her and Maddie to get off the mountain. Maybe this one time....

"Mom, we'll be just fine, I promise." Rachael tried to convince her mother that she had no feeling of impending danger and that she and Maddie were well-stocked and determined to stay in their house above Silver Creek. They'd been doing well on their own and were not afraid.

Edna offered her another cup of coffee and shook her head.

Rachael refused the coffee. "No thanks, Mom." She smiled at Maddie, who sat on an oval rug and played with her doll in the warmth of the wood stove.

"Well, honey," Edna continued, "Your dad and I just think it'd be a good idea for y'all to stay down here for a couple of days. Just 'til we see what the weather's gonna do. You know that Myrtle Ward's been callin' for somethin' fierce to hit and—"

Rachael rolled her eyes. "Mom, Myrtle Ward's been saying that one day the Tye River is going to flood and take everyone and everything in its path, and it hasn't happened yet."

"Well, Rachael, that's not to say it won't some-day."

Rachael shrugged. "I'm not going to be scared out of my home. If it really starts to look bad, we'll come down, but I've got work to do and we need to get on the road." She arose from her chair and pulled on her coat. "Come on, Maddie. Get your coat."

The little girl jumped up and put her doll back in its place in the hall closet.

Edna helped Maddie with her coat and scarf. She

gave her a kiss and hugged her. "Now, you take care of yourself, sweetie, and talk your mama down the mountain if it gets to doin' anything much, you hear?"

"Don't worry about us, Gramma. We're mountain girls." She looked at her mother and winked, then kissed her grandmother on the cheek and went outside.

Rachael hugged her mother. "I know you worry, Mom, but we'll be fine, really." She walked to the door and looked out. Maddie was waiting in the car.

Edna squeezed her daughter's shoulder and kissed her temple. "You just keep an eye on the weather, honey, you hear me?"

"I will," Rachael answered as she stepped out the house. "If we don't see Daddy, tell him we'll be all right. Don't let him come up there and make me feel helpless." Rachael opened the car door and got in. She started the car and honked the horn.

Maddie waved goodbye to her grandmother and blew her a kiss as her mother backed out of the driveway....

Paul was about to turn left onto the main road when he saw his daughter's green Ford coming his way. He cut off the truck's engine and stepped out onto the dirt road.

Rachael pulled off the hard-surface road and brought her car to a stop.

As she rolled down her window, Maddie reached across her and leaned out to kiss her grandfather. "Hi, Papa," she said with a big smile.

"How's my girl?" Paul kissed her cheek and forehead and pulled playfully at the long, brown hair that fell around her face.

"Mama and I have been to the store and to see Gramma." Maddie backed over to her seat on the passenger's side of the car. "She said that you want us to stay there for a few days, but you know we just can't, on account that we're mountain girls, and we're tough!"

Rachael patted her daughter on the knee. "All right, Maddie, don't overdo it." She looked at her father and smiled. "Dad, we'll be fine, and I promised Mom that if it starts to get bad, we'll come on down."

Paul kicked the dirty whitewall tire of his daughter's car as if he was thinking of what to say.

Rachael and Maddie watched him.

Finally he spoke. "Well, them tires ain't got much grip without chains, and you know that road up there ain't more than a varmint's trail."

"I know," Rachael admitted, "but if it starts to really come down, we'll be careful." She looked at her father as if asking for permission.

He knew he could never win when she looked at him like that. He grinned a little and bent down and kissed her on the cheek. "You best do just that," he warned in his most serious tone. "I'm headin' out to walk a stretch of Buck Engle's woods. Just saw Beecher, and he's fine and 'bout as stubborn as you. Said y'all were comin' up there."

Rachael nodded, "We've got a bag of flour for him, and Maddie wants to visit."

Paul leaned into the car and winked at his granddaughter. "You gonna take care of your mama and make her mind?" he asked in a playful voice.

The little girl flashed her perfect white teeth, then reached back across her mother and kissed her grandfather's cool face. She detected a hint of Beecher's scent about him, a mixture of sweet tobacco and wood smoke. "I'll keep her in line, Papa," she assured him with a determined voice.

Paul touched her small fingers with his, then pushed away from the car. He looked up at the cloudy sky. "Air's damp and the temperature's fallin'. If it lets loose, it'll snow." He looked at Rachael and raised his brow. The look was familiar to her, and she knew he was serious.

"I'll watch it, Daddy," she said in a promising tone.

Paul climbed into his truck and started the engine. He waved and watched his daughter pull away. Maddie blew him a kiss that he pretended to catch. He watched the car in his rear-view mirror until it disappeared around the bend. Then he drove out onto the main road. Buck Engle's place was only a few miles away....

Beecher Whitman pulled back the screen from his fireplace and loosened the tobacco ash in the bowl of his pipe with the small blade of his pocket knife. He tapped the pipe on the iron grate and emptied its contents into the mound of hardwood ashes. He hadn't burned a fire in the large fireplace for almost a week and had closed off the draft. The combination wood and cook stove which sat on a shallow, but wide, stone platform in the middle of the great room was far more heat-efficient. He had explained the idea for its design to Ezra Troyer, who was one of the finest stonemasons in the area. The large stove was situated within a thick, three-sided stone structure, one and a half feet in height at either end, with a wall at the back which sloped up from the rear corners into a heavy four-cornered chimney. The chimney, which contained an eight-inch flue, pierced the cathedral ceiling of the cabin at its center. The iron stove was of solid construction, and the heat it radiated through the cabin was sufficient even on the coldest of days. The stone base was a safety measure which allowed Beecher the assurance that a fallen coal from a fire wouldn't ignite the wood floor. Nevertheless, he was always extremely careful.

Beecher returned the screen to its place in front of the fireplace and laid a couple of pinches of dark tobacco in his pipe bowl. He tamped it gently with his finger, put the stem to his lips, and struck a match on a stone above the fire screen. He brought the little flame to his pipe and drew until the warm and fragrant smoke came into his mouth. He threw the match into the cold fireplace and returned to his work table.

The man sat down and picked up the carving on which he had been working for the past four days. It felt good in his strong hands. With his fingers he traced the curves of its body, the details of its features, and its outstretched hands. He touched a splinter near the top of a wing and carefully made it disappear with the razor-sharp blade of his penknife. A small, thin groove in the wood, which in the carver's mind was a sheer drapery covering the angel's nakedness, was not quite deep enough. So Beecher reached over to the window seat where there lay an array of u-shaped gouges, v-tools, and chisels. He settled on a small-bladed veiner. Meticulously he placed the blade against the groove of the pine sage wood and pressed it firmly with his thumb, while following the arc of the groove. With this motion he extracted only a small, thin strand of wood; however, the result was perfect. He used the veiner in two other places before he was satisfied.

Again he felt the carving from the tip of its wings to its base. He counted the small fingers on each hand and the toes on its feet. And when finally he was satisfied, he brought it to his face. He laid his pipe in a clay dish on the table and breathed in the fragrance of the pine wood. He knew it was unlike the others which were carved from the heartwood of the yellow poplar. They were light to pale cream in color. And they were beautiful. This angel was white.

"Hello, my angel," whispered the carver. "Now you exist, as in my dream, and I will keep you separate from the others until I know where it is you must go." He brought the angel to his lips and kissed its head. Then he pulled a shallow tray of fine sand in front of him and began smoothing his creation even more with his fingers and the loose granules. He was careful not to erase the definitions made by his blades.

As the carver worked, he thought about his dreams and his past. He remembered the night long ago when he made a promise to his newborn baby sister. The man whispered, "Don't you worry none, little sister. Beecher's got something pretty to watch over you." But he had been too late. He had prayed for his sister to be all right. And he had carved her a little angel that looked like one he had seen in a dream. But later that night so long ago when he had laid the angel on the bed beside her, he realized she had died.

A sadness had come over the boy and his parents that only time would diminish. But for young Beecher Whitman there was something worse than sadness. Locked into his heart was an element of guilt. He accepted this undeserved burden and made a silent vow that he would never be too late again. All the newborn children he heard of became his sisters and brothers, and he carved for them the angels of his dreams. He never signed his angels, and no one around Tyro knew for sure just who the angel carver was. Not his parents or even his best friend, Paul Tanner. And when he returned home blinded from the war, who would ever have believed that he could again create such beautiful works of art? But Beecher once had the gift of sight, and his memories were indelible. His determination to live his life was strong, so with the help of his parents and his friend, he learned to be self-reliant. He could do just about everything except drive a vehicle.

After the passing of his parents, he continued to live in the hollow given his name, where the forest and the mountains were his friends. He seldom ventured into the village, but was known to come to the Tea Room at times to chat and deliver a bag of his carvings. Word got around fast among the folks in Tyro and Massie's Mill, and whenever Beecher came down from his hollow, the Tea Room would fill with old friends and children eager to see him and buy his carvings. But never in his bag were there angels, and no one ever saw one for sale, although there was hardly a household around the area that didn't cherish one or more. Just how the angels were delivered was a mystery to everyone.

And so it became a thing of legend. Some folks thought they knew the truth, and others could not even imagine it.

Beecher Whitman knew it, although he felt no obligation to admit it. So the angels came from one man's dreams and into the homes of newborn children. And with each delivery there was a prayer of thanks to the angel carver, whoever he might be, for it was he who sent the winged ones to watch over the children. The message was clear....

Beecher smoothed his angel as he thought about his dream of her. She had come to him much as the others had, lacing his thoughts with words and images so profound and vivid that he could never forget. She told him that her name was Hannah and that, unlike the others who had come to watch over the new births, she was the angel of rebirth. She was larger than the other angels and her beauty was exquisite. Her eyes were like diamonds that refracted the sparkle of a thousand stars. Her wings were like long, thin clouds that swirled the air above her head and rippled the light gown that swept beneath her heels. Her face was almost too beautiful to behold, and her hands moved gracefully with her words. "A soul is lost and drifting," she had told the carver in his dream.

"But what am I to do?" he asked.

"Follow the voice of your heart in all things."

"Who needs my help, Angel?"

"The name is in the storm. A voice crying in the wind. Listen and you will know it. A life lies in the strength of your faith, Carver. Believe in it even when all around you are lame of heart."

The beautiful angel had then touched the shoulders of Beecher. As she drifted away, she added, "Keep me for this one whom you will know."

The wind swept the treetops outside Beecher's cabin, and the woodcarver heard a dead limb hit the tin roof and slide off into a brown carpet of leaves. He stood up and draped a thin cloth over the angel. "Come on, Hannah," he said. He walked to a cabinet at the far end of the great room and pulled open a door. On the shelves inside were eleven carved angels. No two angels were alike. He set Hannah apart from the others and was about to close the cabinet door, when he heard footsteps on the front porch. He left the cabinet door slightly ajar and started to the front door.

"Hello, Beech." It was Rachael.

He smelled the fragrance of her hair and would have known who it was even without hearing her voice.

She closed the door behind her and pulled a strand of hair out of her face. "I brought you some flour," she said as she placed the bag in his hands. "And Jim Gresby said to tell you 'Hi' and to give you this." She tucked the envelope into his breast pocket.

Beecher took the bag of flour and gave her a quick hug. "Thank you, Rachael," he said, then smiled as he asked, "Where's the boss?"

Rachael hugged him back and grasped his strong forearm. They walked toward the kitchen. "She saw a chipmunk and chased it around back. But don't worry. The chipmunk had a good head start."

Beecher chuckled. "I was so busy I didn't even hear you drive up," he said, while putting away the flour.

Rachael was in the process of filling three mugs with tea. "Uh, oh," she laughed. "You're slipping. I thought you could hear the car engine when it turns off the main road." She put a little honey in Beecher's and Maddie's tea and a spoonful of white sugar in hers.

"Well, I can unless I'm on some other planet." Beecher walked over to the stove and held out his hand. Rachael took it and said, "Hot." Then she touched his outstretched fingers with the mug handle.

Beecher took the mug and sat down by the stove.

Rachael looked out the back window and saw Maddie heading in from the woods. "Here she comes," she warned.

The door opened and in stepped the little girl. "Beecher Whitman, I got a bone to pick with you!" she said loudly, her hands on her hips.

Surprised, the man turned his face to the girl. "What did I do?" he questioned.

Maddie stepped closer to him. "You got all these squirrels and chipmunks running around outside, and there's not a grain of nothin' in your feeders."

Beecher hung his head for a moment in shame. "Oh, Maddie. I've been too busy to think about the critters today," he admitted. "Tell you what," he started.

"What?" Maddie demanded.

"Well, I'll give you a dime if you forgive me and scatter a little corn in the feeders for me."

The girl wrapped her arms around Beecher's neck and kissed him on the cheek. "You're forgiven," she said as she hurried across the room to the grain bag which sat in the corner beside the wood bin. She picked up the half-filled bag and hurried out the door.

Rachael, who had stood near the stove warming her hands, watched her daughter leave the room, then noticed the wood chips on the table next to the window.

"What did you carve today, Beech?" she asked while looking around. The shelves which lined the walls of the cabin were filled with his carvings. There were wooden animals and birds. He had even carved a school of bream, their bodies protruding at the end of thin twigs as if they were darting in all directions. A black bear leaning forward, his paws on a tree trunk, caught her eye. That was one of her favorites. It was on the shelf with his painted carvings, ones she had painted for him. She walked over and sat in a chair next to him. "Gosh, Beech, don't ever sell," she teased. "You might make some money."

The man smiled. "If you're talking about that bear, you can forget it, lady. It's my favorite."

She reached over and patted his hand. "Just kidding, Beecher. I don't like to see any of them go."

Maddie came in and dropped the grain bag in the corner. She took off her coat and pulled her journal and a pencil out of her pocket. She sat down at

Beecher's work table and pushed the sand tray and carving chips out of her way. Then without a word, she began to write. Beecher could hear the lead of her pencil glide across the paper.

"That little girl's gonna write a book one day," he mused.

Rachael agreed. "She loves to write her stories. Sometimes she reads them to me before she goes to bed."

Beecher chuckled. "She's in her own world, isn't she?"

Rachael looked over at her daughter. "Don't let her fool you," she warned. "She hears everything that goes on around her and is pretty perceptive for a seven-year-old."

Maddie cut her eyes at her mother and grinned.

Rachael turned her head back to Beecher. "I heard on the radio that there's a big front coming in on us. They say we might get some snow out of it."

Beecher didn't speak. He just nodded his head as if in thought.

Rachael continued, "Mom and Dad are about to have a fit for us to come down to the house for a few days. They say Myrtle Ward is predicting a blizzard." She waited.

Still, Beecher didn't say anything. He sipped his tea and felt his breast pocket for his pipe. Suddenly, he felt it placed in his hand by cool little fingers. "Thank you, Maddie," he said as he filled the pipe bowl with tobacco. He lit it, not caring if he drew smoke. The little girl returned to her writing and he to his listening.

"Well, Beech, what do you think? Is it going to snow?"

Quietly the man responded, "Probably."

Rachael had played this kind of game with him before. "Will it be a blizzard?"

Beecher drew a little thin tobacco smoke and answered, "Could be."

And then the woman asked the question he knew was coming. "Well, do you think we ought to go down to the house or not?"

He smiled and answered, "Now, Rachael, I know that you're just as stubborn about that sort of thing as I am and the only way you'd leave is if your house burned down, God forbid, and then you'd probably walk up here." He let some of what he had said sink in before he continued. "So here's what I'm going to advise. If for some strange reason your stubborn side takes leave of you and you decide to go, then do it before the weather gets too bad."

Rachael puckered her lips, squinted her eyes, and crossed her arms. "And what about you, Beecher Whitman? What will you be doing?"

Beecher intended to be smug. "Who, me? Well, I'll just be doing fine, thank you."

Maddie burst out laughing. "You should have known he'd say that, Mama!"

Beecher chuckled.

Rachael scowled playfully at her daughter. "That's enough," she said.

Maddie closed her journal and walked over to a bookshelf. She searched for only a moment, then pulled out a small, green, hardbound volume of poems. She opened it and began to read to herself.

"I told you, Beech," Rachael reminded him. "She doesn't miss a thing."

"Wonder where she got that from?" Beecher teased.

Rachael got up and took their empty tea mugs over to the kitchen sink. "Guess I'm it," she said as she began rinsing them out.

Maddie quickly moved over and took her mother's chair. She turned to a poem and began reading it aloud.

Rachael looked around and listened to her daughter.

> I love to tread the solitudes,
> The forests and the trackless woods,
> Where nature, undisturbed by man,
> Pursues her voluntary plan.

Five stanzas of the poem followed until she was interrupted by her mother on the final one—

> I love the busy marts of trade,
> I love the things which men have made,
> Though man has charms, none such as these,
> In him the child of nature sees.

There was a moment of silence after Rachael finished her recitation.

"Nature's Child," she said finally.

Maddie was impressed. "How did you know that, Mama?"

The woman walked over to Beecher as he stood up. "It's from a collection of poetry by a blind man named Alfred Castner King. I read all of his poems, remember, Beech?"

Beecher nodded and smiled. "I remember well, Rachael."

Rachael looked at the man before her. He was tall and strong and as gentle as a spring breeze. In her eyes he was most handsome. She had always thought so, even with the scars around his eyes. Like Maddie, she looked past them. She had known him all her life, had run up into the hollow on warm summer days as a child and read books to him on his front porch. And he had taught her things she would never forget about the nature of the forest, the animals, and people. He had given her so much of himself and asked for nothing in return. To her, he was greater than any legend a storyteller could imagine. And he had always been there for her.

When her husband died and people reached out to her with kind words and advice, only Beecher said and did the right thing. He guided her without preaching and consoled her without smothering her. He accepted her the way she was, adrift in her grief, and allowed her the space to become what she could be again. Rachael Lundy was not yet whole. But she was where she needed to be. She did know that. And in her heart she knew something else.

She cleared her throat. "Maddie," she spoke, "put the book back and put your coat on. We've got to get home."

Maddie walked back to the bookshelf.

"Beech," Rachael's voice was soft and emotional.

"Yes, Rachael."

She swallowed and moved closer to him. "To me there is one exception to the end of that poem."

Beecher didn't say anything.

"You," she whispered with trembling lips.

Maddie scooted the chair back under Beecher's work table and threw on her coat and scarf. "Ready," she called. "Let's go."

As her mother put on her coat, Maddie walked over and hugged Beecher. She reached out her hand and pulled her mother into their embrace, and together they felt the security of Beecher's strong arms.

Later as they drove down the hill to their house, Maddie asked, "When you were a little girl, how old was Beecher, Mama? Was he old enough to be your father?"

"Well, honey, he's a few years younger than Dad," Rachael answered, thinking how time changes one's perception of age. Yes, she thought. Once, she had perceived Beecher Whitman to be almost like a father to her, and she had loved him as such. But that seemed so long ago, and now things were different. Her heart fluttered as she realized her desire.

Up the hill another heart fluttered as Beecher rubbed his sweaty palms on his britches. He tried to calm himself with a cup of hot tea, but it practically sloshed out of his mug. He thought that eating a biscuit would help, but when he reached for the basket, he knocked it over and listened as his fluffy little snacks rolled onto the floor in all directions. Finally, he just sat down in his chair by the stove for his own safety. He had spent the last few years in denial, avoiding the idea that what had just happened was even remotely possible. But now a door was opened and it led into a room where Beecher Whitman had never been....

Paul Tanner finished pumping gas into his truck's tank and looked through the front window of the Tea Room. He saw Jim Gresby at his usual place at the end of the counter next to the cash register. A minute later when he opened the door and stepped into the store, he was met with the stifling heat from the wood stove. Charley Druen and Rudd Clary were playing a game of pool and old Lemus Boford sat close to the stove in his rocking chair, nursing a steaming cup of coffee.

"Hey, Paul, what can I do you for?" Jim folded his newspaper and put his hand on the counter.

Paul pulled out his wallet and handed the store keeper two dollars. "Got a dollar fifty worth, Jim."

Jim reached into the change tray and took out two quarters. He handed the coins to Paul and closed the register drawer. "Been listenin' to the radio and they say there's a massive front movin' in. We ain't in the center, but we're pretty close." Jim leaned against the end of the counter. "We're liable to get six inches to a foot of snow, with heavy winds."

Paul raised his eyebrows. He felt dampness forming around his neck, and he loosened his collar. "Lemus, how do you stand that heat?" he asked.

The old man was dressed in denim overalls, leather work boots, a flannel shirt, and an old ragged wool coat he'd probably worn for thirty years. His brown fedora was pushed back on his head, and there wasn't a bead of perspiration on him.

Lemus leaned back in his rocker and chuckled. "Old bones, Paul."

Paul Tanner walked past the old man and stood next to the side door of the building. It had been left partially open, and he could see the Gresby house across the yard. He spoke to Charley and watched Rudd sink a six ball in a corner pocket.

"Had to leave that door open," Charley volunteered. "Billy Gump came by earlier today, and the stench 'bout chased us out of here."

Paul thought he could still detect the scent of Billy, and he fanned the door back and forth a few times. The fresh air was good.

"Who's winnin'?" he asked.

Charley cut his eyes at Rudd and sighed, "Ain't really no game. We're just shootin'. But if it was real, I'd be losing, I reckon."

Rudd sank the seven ball in a side pocket. "'Bout

same as always, Paul. How you gettin' on?"

Paul walked toward the front door as he spoke. "Doin' all right, Rudd. Don't you be too hard on ol' Charley."

"I seen some snow in my time," Lemus volunteered as Paul walked by him. He wanted to leave, but he knew that Lemus Boford didn't usually say much, and when he did, it was brief; so he paused at the counter next to Jim.

"I'll bet you have, Lemus."

The old man nodded his head once and started, "I seen some hard winters 'round here, but back in '84, I was a young man in Farmville when we had us a big 'un. Got called out to a place called Stanley Park where a Mr. Twelvetrees' place done caught fire. Snow was so deep we had us a time just gettin' to the place. Couldn't save the house, and the only way we saved the outbuildings was by throwin' snow on 'em. It was a mess, and that fella lost 'bout all he had." Lemus coughed and cleared his throat. "Had a blizzard there in '99, too. It was the year 'fore I come back to the mountains. Snow was up to your knees. And you could step in a drift up to your waist. I recollect it was hard on folks."

Jim Gresby spoke up, "What do you think about the forecast, Lem?"

Lemus huffed. "Can't nobody call it for sure better'n fifty-fifty. When you stock up for one, it don't come, and when you don't, it do. You get the worst trouble when you don't respect the cold and what it can do. I seen fellas lose their fingers and toes to frostbite 'fore they know'd it." Lemus gulped the rest of his coffee. "If it comes a snow, well, then that's all right. But if we get a blow with it, then that's a blizzard. And a blizzard's a demon."

Charley and Rudd had stopped their playing and were listening to Lemus. Rudd turned up his cola bottle and finished his drink. He set the bottle down on the edge of the pool table and laid his pool stick in its rack on the wall. "Come on, Lemus," he said, putting on his coat. "Let me run you home before you bring a scare on us."

Lemus rose slowly from his chair and fumbled with the buttons on his coat. "Well, now, I'm just a'tellin' y'all what I seen." That was all he said.

Paul rapped his knuckles on the counter top and moved to the door. "I'll see y'all later," he said as he opened the door.

They spoke their farewells, and Paul stepped outside ahead of Rudd and Lemus. The cold, damp wind bent down the soft brim of his felt hat as he bowed his head into it and made his way to the truck.

Inside the Tea Room, Charley Druen closed the side door and racked up the balls for a little practice. Jim Gresby turned up his radio. Bob Conley's orchestra was on. He looked up at the big clock on the wall. Betty would walk over with their supper at 6 o'clock, just in time for the news. It was their nightly routine to listen to Amos 'n' Andy and Lum an' Abner. After Blondie went off, they'd close the store and walk across the yard to their house.

Jim watched as Paul Tanner pulled his truck onto

the road. Then he opened his paper and resumed reading about the war in Europe. That was a distant storm....

Rachael looked at the calendar which hung on the wall above the breakfast table in her kitchen. It was four years to the day since Michael had died. She finished drying the few dishes she had washed after supper and peeked around the doorway into the living room. Maddie was writing in her journal. Rachael opened a cabinet door and put two plates back in their places. She hung the dish towel on a rack above the sink and looked out the kitchen window in the direction of Beecher's cabin. What would Michael think, she wondered. Through her, he had come to know Beecher and realized what an important person he was in her life. He had even enjoyed visiting with the older man and found him most interesting. What had baffled him most was how Beecher could walk the Big and Little Priest mountains without becoming lost. "It's unbelievable!" he used to say.

But Rachael would remind him that Beecher had once been able to see and had known the mountains as he knew his own cabin and that after the war had taken his sight, he insisted on knowing the mountains in darkness just as he had known them when he could see. His father had hiked with him every day until age prevented it.

In the early years of their daily travels, the older man led his son, but it wasn't long before he began to follow in amazement. Beecher had known the mountains in his youth, but when he lost his sight, they became a part of his soul. Each step he took and every tree and fold was impressed upon his mind. In his abilities to touch and smell, he had regained what men born of modern civilization had sadly lost. His attention to detail and the acuteness of his senses became the chords of his life. And he was attuned to them in a way that only the blind can know. Beecher Whitman had not let fate ruin him, for it was not his character to crawl beneath the blanket of self-pity. It was a strong faith and a stubborn determination that drove Beecher beyond life's encumbrances. These characteristics gave him sight beyond seeing.

Rachael felt in her heart that Michael would understand her feelings. Her parents? Well, they would question only the years between them and, after a while, that would become moot.

For a moment she felt silly. She was full of questions that concerned the convictions of two people. She knew her own feelings, but was it only her imagination that he felt the same way about her?

Since the death of her husband, she had come to depend on Beecher in ways unknown to all but perhaps Maddie. Seldom a day would go by that she and her daughter didn't see him, and lately he had seemed to show up at her door more frequently. He would never stay long and preferred to visit out on the porch. During warm weather, the three of them went for walks. Sometimes the distances were great, and it would be hours before they returned home. They'd fish and picnic and play games of memory.

Beecher always encouraged Maddie to write her little stories, and he loved to listen to them. "You're going to write a book one day," he'd tell her. Her love for him was obvious, and his influence could not have been better. If Beecher had faults, he kept them to himself.

What had developed between Rachael and Beecher was rooted in a trusted friendship. Such a thing is not diminished by years and, in its truest form, is a treasure.

The last few years had been hard on Rachael's emotions. She had loved her husband dearly. When he was taken so early in their marriage, she was left with many questions, questions that troubled her soul and shook the very foundation of her faith. There were few answers. Her passion was her painting, and between that and Maddie there was little room for anything or anyone else. She did not attend church or community functions and only took part in art exhibits when necessary. She had kept Maddie out of first grade because of what she called the child's emotional immaturity, but she knew in her heart that it was her own fear of letting the child go. Beecher had told her, "If you continue to shield her from the world, her wonder will fade into angry questions, and the light in her heart will be dimmed. The outside will become like a monster, and in her fear to live she will die a little each day."

Rachael knew he was speaking not only of her daughter but also of her. That realization had begun a slow change in her, for it was not her desire that Maddie should suffer. She knew that she would have to enroll the child in school in the fall, and she knew also that she would have to commit herself again to the world outside. But it was so hard, and the emotional stumbling blocks were many.

"I'm sleepy, Mama."

Rachael turned and saw Maddie standing in the doorway, rubbing her eyes. She went to her daughter and hugged her. "I'm sorry, honey. I was lost in my thoughts. Did you finish your story?"

Maddie looked troubled. "I don't know how to end it yet."

Her mother smiled. "It'll come. Don't worry about it. The best writers in the world have to wait for a little inspiration sometimes." She put her hand on the child's shoulder and guided her to her bedroom. "Come on, let's get to bed. We might see a little snow tomorrow."

Minutes later, she tucked a quilt around Maddie's shoulders, and as she leaned over, she touched the little girl's nose with her finger and looked into her sleepy brown eyes. "We're going to be all right, Maddie. Don't you worry."

Maddie lifted her arms out from under the quilt

and put them around her mother's neck. She pulled her close. "And Gramma and Papa?"

"Yes."

"And Beecher?"

Rachael smiled. "Yes, and Beecher, too." She kissed the child and covered her again. "Now say your prayers and go to sleep. I'll be working for a while."

Maddie smiled and turned on her side.

Her mother turned off the oil lamp and went into the next room where she prepared to resume work on a painting she had begun that morning.

Maddie watched her for a while, then closed her eyes and said a prayer. Soon she was sound asleep....

It was mid-morning before the Lundy household awoke. Rachael had almost finished her painting when fatigue overtook her in the wee hours of the morning. She had fallen asleep on the couch.

"Mama." Maddie's voice was soft. She yawned.

Rachael opened her eyes and focused on her daughter. "Good morning," she said, stretching her arms.

"It's snowing, Mama."

Rachael turned her head and looked out the window. "You're right." She opened her eyes wide and sat up. "It sure is." She slipped her feet into her shoes, then draped her blanket around Maddie's shoulders. There was a chill in the house.

"We overslept, honey," she told her daughter.

Maddie settled back into the warm place on the couch left by her mother. She pulled the soft blanket up around her and stared out the window.

Rachael opened the door to the wood stove and raked the coals flat with a short-handled shovel. The heat felt good on her face. She opened a closet door and retrieved an old corduroy coat. It was worn, and a patch on one of the elbows was torn. She put it on and reached into a pocket for a pair of gloves.

Maddie noticed how the coat hung off her mother's shoulders. The sleeves were too long, and it somehow made her mother look like a petite and beautiful tramp.

Rachael pulled on her gloves and looked over at the child. "If I don't find my way back, don't worry. There's food in the icebox."

Maddie smiled. The wood was stacked at the back door. She watched as her mother opened the door and stepped out. A cold blast of air found its way across the room and caused her to shiver under her blanket.

Rachael was outside for less than a minute, but when she reentered the house with three logs, she was covered with snow. She placed the logs in the stove and opened the dampers. "There now," she said, while removing her coat. "That will get some heat going for us." She opened the back door and shook the snow off the coat as best she could, then closed the door and hung the coat on the back of a chair to dry. "That wind is something. Feels like it's blowing right through you." She walked into the kitchen to begin breakfast. "Maddie," she called, "you wear flannel under your bibs today. That wind is going to make it hard to keep the house warm. You hear?"

Maddie could smell bacon frying as she reached into her drawer for her clean flannel pajamas. She dressed slowly, and when she had finished, looked at herself in the mirror. "Papa's right," she complained out loud. "I look like a boy who needs a haircut." She pulled her long brown hair behind her head and slipped a band around it, then repeated herself in a deeper voice. She made a face at her reflection and left the room.

Breakfast was an omelet with cheese and bacon, a piece of hot buttered toast and jam and a glass of milk. Maddie liked to eat in silence, but it seldom happened because her mother was in the habit of listening to the radio whenever she was in the kitchen. This particular morning, the volume was up a little louder than usual, and the announcer was going on about the storm which had come up from the south and entered Virginia in its southwest section. Already, Bristol had nine inches of snow on the ground and, closer to home, Lynchburg had six inches and Staunton, four. Roanoke and Lexington had about a half foot of snow. Roads were becoming impassable, and schools had already canceled classes in those areas. It was 24 degrees outside, but the wind made it seem much colder, and the radio announcer warned against prolonged exposure outdoors. The storm was settling in, it seemed, and its center was close by.

When Kate Smith began to sing a song, Rachael turned the volume down and started clearing the table. "Myrtle Ward might be right this time."

"Are we gonna go down to Gramma's and Papa's house, Mama?" Maddie brought her dishes to the sink.

Rachael looked out the kitchen window before answering. "I think we'll go down shortly. I want to finish my painting first." She looked down at her daughter. "Are you scared, honey?"

Maddie shrugged her shoulders and fanned the dish towel before taking a wet plate from her mother. "I've seen snow before, Mama." She placed the dry plate on the counter. "If it makes them feel better for us to be there, it's fine with me. But Beecher will sure be lonely up here all by himself."

"He's weathered a lot of storms up here, Maddie. And I don't think I've ever heard him complain about being lonely."

"Well, does he want us to go?"

Rachael pulled the stopper out of the sink and rinsed the frying pan. "I think he would feel better knowing we were with Mom and Dad until this is over."

"Did he say that, Mama?"

Rachael smiled and looked out the window. "Yes, he said it in his own way."

After their late breakfast, Rachael and Maddie

buried themselves in their projects. Maddie rearranged her room (an effort that had become a weekly routine) and reread books she had been given for Christmas. She wrote in her journal and tried in vain to conjure up the finest of all endings for her story. But after searching her thoughts for so long a time, she became tired and fell asleep.

Rachael entered the world of her imagination and faded away from the present until the final stroke of her paint brush brought to fruition that which she had desired. The day passed quickly.

The wind outside the Lundy house blew across the hollow and strengthened its force until weakened tree branches began to break and crash to the ground as if thrown by some angry giant. Nearby an ancient chestnut tree, killed years before by a foreign blight, began to tilt. Finally its roots snapped under the strain of its weight, and the forest skeleton which had stood almost one hundred feet tall fell into the surrounding treetops, breaking them like toothpicks. The sound of its violent crash was all but lost in the roar of the wind.

The chestnut tree hit with such force that its great limbs pierced the wood-shingled roof of the Lundy's little frame house like jagged spears. It was as if the inside of the house exploded.

Rachael had just covered her painting and was placing it in the corner of the room when the roof caved in. A tree limb one and a half feet in diameter crashed into the floor beside her. The jolt slammed her against the wall. Window panes burst, and shards of glass became deadly missiles which riddled the walls and furniture. Rachael heard Maddie cry out for her and watched in horror as the tree tilted and settled in the direction of the child's room, its great splintered branches churning up the floor and pulling down the ceiling. The light from the oil lamp by which Rachael had worked was extinguished by a downward blast of wind which screamed through the house, scattering snow and debris everywhere.

"No! Oh, God, no!" Rachael climbed onto the fallen tree, but could not find an open passage to Maddie's bedroom. The walls along the short hallway that separated the two rooms had collapsed into rubble. Rachael called out loud, "Hold on, Maddie. I'm coming around to your window." With that, she half fell, half slid off the wet tree and groped her way toward the kitchen. She tripped over a chair and fell to the floor. Reaching out, she felt the collar of the coat she had worn earlier. She sat up and pulled on the coat, buttoning it as she got to her feet.

In the kitchen, plates and glasses had fallen out of the cabinets and lay scattered and broken on the floor. She felt them crunch beneath her shoes. The room was otherwise spared from damage, and soon Rachael's fingers grasped the car keys that hung on a wooden spike next to the door. She shoved them in her coat pocket and pulled open the door. Snow and bitter wind forced her to lower her face as she hurried outside. She winced at the sting of snow and sleet on her forehead. The wind blew almost horizontally. The fallen chestnut tree loomed out of the swirling snowfall, and Rachael could barely see where it lay prostrate upon the house. She hunched under it, then made her way to the window outside her daughter's room. Putting her face to a broken glass pane, she called at the top of her voice. At first there was no response. She called out Maddie's name again. Fear rose in her heart, until a small hand reached out and touched her face. "Mama, are you all right?" Maddie's voice was anxious.

Rachael put the child's hand to her lips and cried, "Yes, yes, I'm all right. Are you hurt?" She could hardly make out the outline of her daughter's face.

"There's a big tree in my room, Mama!"

"I know, Maddie." Rachael was thinking and searching the ground around her while she talked. She reached down and picked up a broken limb the size of a baseball bat. She had tried to push up the window, but it was off its track and wouldn't budge.

"Listen to me, Maddie," she called. "Pull the blanket off your bed if you can and wrap it around you. Stand over in the corner. I'm going to knock the window out so I can get you out of there."

Maddie had already found her shoes and put them on. She felt for her journal on the bed and put it in her pocket, then pulled the soft woolen blanket off the foot of her bed and draped it around her shoulders. She stood to the side of the window. "Okay, Mama, I'm out of the way. Hit it!"

Rachael reared back and swung the stick, shattering the window. She didn't stop until she had cleared the frame of glass and splinters, then she threw the stick into the snow and reached in for Maddie. "Come on, baby," she called. "Let's get out of here!"

Maddie climbed onto the window frame and practically fell into her mother's arms. "I knew you'd come and get me, Mama," she said, hugging her mother's neck.

Rachael leaned against the house and buried her face in the child's caress. She put her lips to Maddie's ear. "You've got to be strong, honey. We're going to walk to the car and go down the mountain. But you've got to stay with me and be brave."

"I'm with you, Mama. Let's go!"

Rachael put the girl down and led her by the hand. The wind-driven snow made it almost impossible to see more than a few feet ahead, but Rachael stayed close to the house and led Maddie back under the tree. When they got to the kitchen door, Rachael paused to get her bearings. She could not see the car from where they stood, but she knew it was there, just beyond the graveled walkway.

Questions rang in Rachael's thoughts. Should they remain in the house where they might freeze to death? Could they make it up the mountain and over to Beecher's cabin? She knew they had to try to get to safety. The house was ripped apart. They couldn't survive there. Myrtle Ward had called it right this time. The blizzard had come, and no one knew what sudden danger it had brought to Rachael and Maddie Lundy.

Rachael led her daughter away from the house, searching through squinted eyelids for the outline of the car. She practically walked into it before she even realized it was in front of her. She felt for the handle and jerked the door open. "Get in, Maddie," she commanded.

When both of them were inside and the door was closed, Rachael rubbed her face with her hands and pulled Maddie close to her. She started the car and turned on the headlights. "Too much snow," she said. "Wait a minute." She opened the door and stepped out.

Maddie watched as her mother pushed the snow off the windshield. Rachael reached in and switched on the wipers. They struggled and scraped across the icy glass. Next, the woman hurried to the rear of the car and kicked snow away from the back tires. She tried to clear out two tracks down to the gravel so that the tires could find traction. When she had done her best, she got back into the car. Maddie had turned on the heater and the warmth felt good.

"Okay, honey, let's see what she'll do."

Rachael put the Ford in reverse and eased off the clutch while touching the gas pedal lightly. To her surprise the car moved back without a problem. Still she was careful. "We'll have to feel our way down," she told Maddie. She could barely make out the narrow driveway.

Maddie crossed her fingers on the dashboard of the car.

Rachael was careful to ease down the mountain. All was going well until she brought the car around a bend and swung out a little too wide. The car began

sliding toward the bank into a ditch. Overcome by panic, Rachael mashed down on the gas pedal.

Maddie fell back in her seat as the car lunged forward. Rachael felt the car sliding out of control and slammed on the brakes. She struggled with the steering wheel to straighten up the wheels, but nothing would stop it. The car's weight was at the mercy of the sleet and snow.

Maddie screamed and braced herself.

"Hold on, Maddie!" Rachael pressed against the steering wheel. Ahead of her was a turn in the narrow road she knew she couldn't make. The impact as the rear bumper of the Ford struck a boulder brought such a jolt to its two occupants that Maddie was thrown onto the floorboard. Rachael lost her grip on the steering wheel as it spun wildly. She was pitched across the seat as the vehicle made a circle in the road and plunged over the edge.

For a moment the Ford was airborne, and in that eerie silence, Maddie felt the hand of her mother. Then the front of the car slammed into a tree and spun down the steep mountainside, missing trees that might have stopped it, until it struck a mound of earth left by an uprooted tree, flipped into the air and landed on its side in an icy pool of Silver Creek.

Maddie was stunned until a splash of water hit her face. Quickly she stood and felt in the darkness for her mother.

Rachael moaned.

"Mama!" Maddie felt her mother's arms and pulled at her. She felt water rising around her ankles.

"Mama, you've got to get up. You'll drown!"

Water was seeping into the car from a broken window. The girl pulled frantically at her mother, but the car seat had dislodged, its full weight holding the woman down.

Rachael felt the water at her back and shoulders. There was pain in her chest, but she spoke calmly, "Maddie, listen to me." She held the child's hand and felt her trembling. "You've got to get help. Do you have your blanket?"

Maddie took a deep breath and answered, "Yes, Mama, it's right here." She gathered it up around her.

"Good, now reach up and roll down the window. Climb out of the car and try not to get wet. The car is in the water." Rachael took short, shallow breaths.

"If I run down the creek bank, I'll come to the bridge, Mama. I can do that." Maddie was shivering from the cold. "I can make it to the Tea Room and get help."

"No, honey. It's too far for you. Run up the creek and get Beecher. You know where it forks?"

"Yes, Mama." Maddie nodded her head in the darkness.

"Good. The little fork to the right takes you up beside the cabin. When you get to the fork, start calling him. Maybe he'll hear you." Rachael gripped the girl's shoulder with her hand, then felt her cold cheek. "Can you do it, honey?"

"I don't want to leave you, Mama," the girl cried.

"You have to, Maddie, or we'll both die."

"But, the water. It's coming in!"

Rachael felt the icy water slurping at her neck.

"Maddie, you have to hurry." She let go of her daughter. "Now, go, honey. Wrap that blanket around you out there and don't stop moving. No matter what, don't stop moving!"

Maddie reached down and felt her mother's face. She kissed her and spoke in her ear. "I'll be back, Mama. You hold on. I love you."

Rachael fought back her tears, for she felt that, even if Maddie could get to safety, her own rescue would be hopeless. It was too cold, and the water was rising steadily. She wasn't sure as to the extent of her injuries, but there was much pain in her chest when she breathed. In her heart, she felt it was the last time she would hear her daughter's voice. She touched the girl's face and felt her lips with her thumb. "I love you, too, Maddie. Don't stop. You have to be strong. Get to Beecher's cabin."

Maddie stood up and reached above her head. She located the small window handle and turned it counterclockwise. Snow fell onto her face. She put the blanket around her shoulders and pulled her body up, using the steering wheel and any footholds she could locate. In a moment, she was perched atop the overturned car. "I'll be back, Mama!" she called. Then she jumped. The sound of her landing on the snow-covered bank of Silver Creek was lost in the storm.

Inside the car Rachael began to pray. The cold water was touching her ears and she began to shiver violently. But still she prayed out loud for her daughter. If only Maddie could be saved. That was all that mattered to her. That was all she asked for....

Maddie had to lift her feet high to move over the snow-covered ground. The wind had piled snow drifts in some places up to her thighs. There she struggled, leaned forward, and waded. Several times she stopped at large trees for refuge from the severity of the snow and sleet that felt like tiny bee stings on her face. She wore the blanket like a hood over her head and held it tight about her neck so that it fell over her shoulders and back and dragged in the snow behind her. At times the wind snatched it and tugged hard at the child. Yet, on she trod, like a tattered vagabond, humble but determined.

She walked, possessed of a single thought—to find the man who could help her. She called out his name, but it was lost in the wind. Her young heart pounded, and she called out the name again, but still the deafening roar of nature's elements stifled her appeal, and she began to doubt herself. Perhaps he would not hear her at all, she thought. The wind was so loud. She might have walked too far, or somehow missed the dry fork of the creek. It was not much more than a stone-lined depression, anyway, devoid of running water except during the heaviest of rains. In such deep snow she could have easily stepped over it without even realizing it. And if that was the case, she would walk on until the blizzard finally defeated her.

Maddie fell against the bole of a tree and began to weep. Long tears burned down her cheeks, tears of hopelessness in the blinding greyness of the storm. Her legs were heavy, but she struggled to stand, remembering the words of her mother. "Don't stop," she told herself. She pushed away from the tree and walked slowly, each step a defiant effort to overcome the fatigue that crept through her body and diminished her will. And then she waded into a snow drift and could not take another step. Maddie looked for the rushing water she had tried to keep so carefully within her sight, but it was gone, lost beyond the veil of snow and wind. Terror seized her heart as she struggled to set herself free of the drift. Her effort was futile. She had become too weak and tired, and in a few seconds, she slumped forward in the snow, her face in her hands.

The angry roar of the wind began to echo as if it were receding into a tunnel. And soon its sound was quieted in her mind, replaced by the cadence of her own heartbeat. A warm feeling began to move through her body, and images drifted before her mind's eye, visions of her mother and grandparents and Beecher, the people she loved most in her young life. Their voices came to her in familiar words. They calmed her. Moments of her life floated before her, and in the distance she heard the faint chiming of bells. Voices mingled until only one voice was audible above all the rest. It was gentle and distinct. And when she heard it, the images in her mind disappeared. "Lift up your head, Maddie, and call out his name," the voice said. The words were unmistakable, soothing, yet powerful.

For moments afterwards, the only sound was of wind chimes, and then the howl of the wind returned, its velocity sweeping the snow in stinging blasts. But still Maddie heard the chimes, and she raised her head and called out as loud as she could, believing in her heart she was not lost. Her strength was in her will to live, her hope in the man whose name she called....

Beecher Whitman reached over and turned off the radio. Bart River's orchestra had already been interrupted twice by storm updates, and the reception was bad. He'd heard the report of treacherous snow drifts on major routes throughout the state. Some highways were impassable. The State Highway Department was unprepared for such a snowfall. Already, drifts of several feet had been reported in a few places. The blizzard that Myrtle Ward had warned of had come and was doing its job well. The central part of the state was practically paralyzed. Beecher had listened all day to the storm outside his cabin as he worked at his table by the window. His mind had been lost in thought at times. Perhaps he should have insisted that Rachael and Maddie leave the mountain. He chewed on his lower lip and sipped from his tea mug. Setting it down on the side table, he rose and walked to the window. It would be dark outside now, he thought, the forest, a no-man's land. He listened. He imagined the bending of the trees, the frightful, blowing curtain of snow and sleet and familiar places made foreign by drifts and fallen debris. He wondered how things were down along the finger ridge. Maddie would be reading or writing in her little book, and Rachael would be at her easel, painting the visions of her imagination. And what an imagination she had!

He remembered how full of wonder she was when she was a young girl. "How do you walk in the woods without falling or bumping into a tree?" she had asked him. "What is it like to be blind?"

Beecher always tried to answer the girl's questions as best he could. He'd recite poetry or passages to her while they sat in chairs on his front porch on languid summer evenings. She loved Emerson and Thoreau and even some of the haunting stories and poems of Edgar Allan Poe. Beecher preferred the nature poems of Alfred Castner King. His father had bought him a copy of King's *Mountain Idylls and Other Poems* and had read it to him often in the years after his son's return from the war. Beecher could relate to the poet as he, too, had been robbed of his sight as a young man. Still, King had been able to find the words in his heart to describe the natural beauty he had known before a mining accident rendered him sightless. Beecher could not write verse, but inspired by King's writings, he taught himself to duplicate the objects of his mind's eye with a carving knife and a block of wood.

Rachael had told him once that his carvings were far better than other wood art she had seen. From each depiction, whether it was in the form of a human or an animal, life emanated. She said it was as if his carvings harnessed the souls of his visions. Beecher had always marveled at the depth of her perception. He knew it would be evident in her paintings. That he had not been able to see her scenes of life on canvas had always caused him regret. But she described her paintings to him in such detail that he could visualize them. He was proud of her success as an artist. And when she had gone away to school, he supported her with confidence. Her visits home were much anticipated, and she always spent time in his company, even after her marriage to Michael Lundy.

Rachael was blessed in a special way, for she had the love of two men. One was her husband, and the other a unique individual who gave so much of himself and expected nothing more than her friendship in return. Rachael loved her husband, but even he knew she adored Beecher. Rachael and Beecher were like kindred spirits, drawn together for reasons unknown. Michael Lundy had loved them both....

Outside, the wind swept across the porch, making the chorus of the chimes continuous. Beecher felt a chill and walked to the stove, opened its door, and with a hand shovel raked a flat place in the glowing coals. From the back of his rocking chair, he took his coat, put it on, and lifted his hat from a rack on the wall next to the front door. He stepped onto the porch, closed the door behind him, and felt the wind in his face. He moved three steps to his right and reached down, filling the cradle of his left arm with firewood. Back in the cabin, he placed the logs in the stove. On a cold, windless night this would have been enough to warm the cabin, but this night he would need to stoke the fire again, so he went back out on the porch for another armful of wood.

It was then as he bent down and felt for the right-sized log that he heard something on the wind. He stood erect and turned his face into the gale. Again he heard it even above the chimes. He placed the log back on the stack of wood and walked to the edge of the porch. Cupping his hands behind his ears, he listened. When again the sound came to him, there was no mistake about it. A child's voice was calling his name, and he knew who the child was.

Beecher's heart began to race. A fear arose within him, and he shouted her name.

Maddie called out again, and the man pinpointed her position.

Beecher grasped the porch rail and stepped down onto the snow-covered ground. He was anxious, even frightened, but not for himself. He wondered what had happened to cause the little girl to be out in such treacherous weather. But there was no time to ponder his fear. He had to get to her, and he concentrated only on her position. She was approximately fifty yards down the hill in front of his cabin where the creek forked. Beecher visualized the forest as he knew it, blocking out the snow that would change its appearance. He knew the trails, the game paths, the flats and folds of the landscape. He could see it in his mind, so when he let go of the porch rail and hurried down the hill, he was not concerned with becoming lost. His only fear was for what he might find.

"Beecher!" Maddie called, her voice becoming hoarse. She held the blanket with one hand at her neck and tried to push herself up on her feet, but it was no use. The strength had gone out of her legs. Staring into the swirling curtain of snow that surrounded her, she called out again. A large tree limb crashed into the snow beside her. The little girl screamed and tried to crawl away from it. She leaned forward and raked at the snow in front of her, but was getting nowhere until all of a sudden she was hoisted up into the strong arms of a man. Maddie looked up and saw his face. "Oh, Beech, I knew you'd come." Her speech was slurred.

Beecher felt her cold face with his hand and

pulled the blanket up around her, cradling her like an infant. "What happened, Maddie?" he shouted over the howling wind.

"It's Mama, Beech. We've got to save her!" Maddie pulled at the breast of his coat.

"Where is she?"

"She's in the car. It went down the hill and turned over in the creek!" The girl was almost hysterical.

Terror raced through Beecher. The mountainside Maddie referred to as a hill was steep, and he could imagine the momentum a vehicle would gain while sliding down it. That the car was in the creek surprised him, as the mountainside had many large trees that should have stopped it.

His first instinct was to rush down the hollow, but he was smarter than that. Instead, he held the girl tightly, turned and hurried back up the hill to his cabin. In a minute he was climbing the porch steps. He flung open the front door and took the child over to the wood stove and pulled the cold blanket off her.

"Are you all right, honey?"

Maddie felt the heat from the stove and huddled next to it. "Yes," she answered. She began to cry. "Beecher, we've got to get Mama out of the car. She's going to drown."

"Drown?" Beecher had jerked another wool blanket off his bed at the far end of the room and rolled it up, then had hurried into a back room and emerged with a length of rope. Returning to Maddie's side, he rubbed her legs vigorously and questioned, "What do you mean, she's drowning?"

Maddie shivered and rubbed her hands together. "The car is on its side, and the seat is on top of Mama. She's hurt, Beecher," the girl sobbed. "She's laying on her back in the water, and—"

Beecher interrupted. "Maddie, let's see if you can stand up." He lifted her to her feet. "There," he said as Maddie stood on her own.

"Here, drink this." Beecher placed his warm mug of tea in her cold hands and guided it to her lips. She drank it quickly.

Beecher tied the rope loosely around his waist, bundled Maddie into a heavy woolen coat, and slipped gloves on her hands. "They're big, but they'll have to do," he said. Then he put his hands on the child's shoulders and spoke to her reassuringly, "We're going to get your mama now, Maddie. You'll ride on old Beecher's back and tell me when we've come to the car. Can you be my eyes?"

"Yes, Beech. Let's go!"

"All right." Beecher bent down and turned his back to the girl. "Now put your legs through the rope and you'll have your own seat back there."

Maddie did as he instructed and locked her hands around his throat, resting her chin on his shoulder.

When she was secure, he stood up and walked to the door. He tucked the wool blanket roll under his arm. Beecher paused for a second before he opened the door. "You gotta be brave, Maddie, no matter what. You ready?"

Maddie held on tight and kissed the man on the neck. "I'm ready, Beech."

With that, Beecher opened the door and in moments was off the porch and heading down the hollow.

In his haste, he failed to close the door of the cabin securely, and the bitter wind found its way in. Papers blew about and window curtains danced wildly. Far to the rear of the great room a cabinet door opened, and a thin rag was lifted into the air, exposing something beautiful, something carved out of the vision of a dream, something that had spoken to the soul of a man....

Rachael tried with all her strength to push the car seat off her, but it was wedged tight and wouldn't budge. For long moments after Maddie had left, she shivered and prayed out loud in slurred speech. The pain along her left rib cage was excruciating. She felt the water rising steadily and lifted her head. She presumed the overturned car had somehow dammed the flow of water running out of the pool. There was no telling how high the water might rise. She struggled to free herself, but her attempt was futile. She knew her only chance was that Maddie could find Beecher, and even then it might be too late. A strange warmth began to come over her body, and her struggles lessened. Her mind wanted her to rise up out of the water, but her body could not react. She thought of Maddie and how frightened her daughter must be. "Oh, God," she whispered, "save her. Save my baby." In her mind, she saw her daughter slumped over in the snow, too weak to get up and walk. It was then that Rachael said the words she could barely form with her lips. "Lift up your head, Maddie, and call out his name." For a while after that she was able to keep her face above the freezing water; but, finally, her last strength waned, and she tried to cough the cold liquid out of her lungs. Her struggle didn't last long, and within seconds her body lay still beneath the blackness, and her soul began to float into a strange place between light and darkness, a place of waiting....

Maddie pounded Beecher's shoulder with her hand. "Stop, Beech," she cried. "Here's the car!"

It had taken a full ten minutes for Beecher to arrive on the scene. The downhill trek was full of such obstacles as fallen tree limbs and even an uprooted tree. Beecher had hurried along a game path beside the icy branch, a game path that was usually clear of debris. Had it not been for Maddie, he would have stumbled and fallen more than once, but the little girl was a good spotter and was able to guide him over and around obstacles.

As he stooped low, she wriggled her legs out of the rope around his waist and called to her mother. There was no answer. She tried to pull away from him and go to the car, but he caught her by the arm. "No, Maddie!" he shouted. "You have to describe it to me. What do you see?"

Maddie strained her eyes. "It's lying on its side with the roof toward us," she said. "Mama is in the back."

"You take this and hold it." Beecher stuffed the wool blanket into the girl's arms. "I'm going to get her out of there. You stay right here."

"Oh, hurry, Beech, hurry!" she pleaded.

Beecher walked toward the car slowly. He stumbled on a root and almost fell, but regained his balance quickly. Cautiously, he stepped out into the water until he could touch the car's roof. The water was just above his knees. He planted his feet firmly and pushed hard against the vehicle. It didn't budge. He called Maddie to the edge of the pool, took off his coat, handed it to her. Then he rolled up his shirt sleeves and reached below the surface of the cold water. He felt around the edge of the submerged roof for a hand hold and worked his fingers between metal and gritty sand until he had a grip. He pulled up with his arms, but could not make the car move. Beecher rose and leaned against the car, his hands numb from the cold. He held them under his arms for warmth. His mind reeled. He fumbled around for something to use as leverage. There was nothing. He turned toward Maddie.

"Pick it up, Beecher. You can do it!" she was crying. "I'll help you!" She started into the water.

Beecher heard her sloshing, reached out and stopped her. "No, Maddie!" he shouted. He walked her back onto the bank. "Now you listen to me." His face was close to hers as he spoke. "I need you to do something for me."

"What?" Maddie was sobbing.

Beecher rubbed his face with numb fingers. "You've got to pray, Maddie. You've got to pray that I can do this. I need you to do that. And you've got to believe it. Can you do that? Because I'm going to pick up that car. I can do it, if we both believe. You hear me?"

"Yes, Beech, I hear you." Maddie sat down in the snow and put her face in her hands as Beecher knelt over her. And together they prayed from their hearts — he for strength and she for a miracle. Their words were different, but their purpose was the same. Unity is born of conviction, and in this there is power.

Beecher went back to the car and reached down into the black swirling water. He found his grip, leaned his body against the roof and pushed with his legs. He felt movement and gave it all his strength.

Maddie was astonished at what she saw. She rubbed her eyes as if doing so would clear her vision. But still she saw it. The car was lifted upright and Beecher opened the rear door carefully, placing his hand against Rachael's back. Water spilled over his thighs into the receding pool as he reached in and with one mighty blow, dislodged the seat which pressed against her ribs. Gently he pulled her cold, lifeless body from the car.

"Spread out the blanket, Maddie," he called as he stepped out of the pool.

Maddie spread out the wool blanket and guided Beecher to it. He lay Rachael down on her back and pulled the blanket over her. Maddie felt her mother's hand and began to cry. "She's gone, Beecher!"

"Give me my coat, Maddie," he demanded, holding out his hand.

Maddie found it in the snow and handed it to him. He shook it and placed it over Rachael's upper torso. Then he put his ear to the woman's mouth and pressed down on the center of her chest. There was a gurgling noise. He pushed down again, harder and blew warm air from his lungs into her mouth while holding her nose with his fingers. "She's waiting, Maddie!" he shouted. "She's waiting to come back. Call her. Call your mama, honey!"

Maddie was so afraid, but she did as Beecher told her. "Come back, Mama!" she cried.

"Touch her, Maddie. Let her know you're here."

The little girl put her hands on her mother's head and called to her over the roar of the wind. She watched as Beecher worked, vigorously pumping her chest and blowing into her mouth.

"Come back to your daughter, Rachael," he pleaded.

"Come back to me!" He bent over and repeated

his last words, then kissed her and blew into her mouth.

Immediately, she coughed, and Beecher turned her slightly on her side. Water spurted out of her mouth as she heaved.

"That's my girl," he told her as he brought her into his arms.

Maddie could not tell if he was crying or laughing. For a moment it seemed as if the blizzard around them had stopped, and in that moment the girl noticed something else, something she would not recall until later. She put her arms around her mother and wept.

Rachael tried to speak, but she couldn't.

Beecher wrapped her tightly in the blanket and turned his face up the mountain toward the house.

Maddie tugged on his sleeve. "Can't go up to the house, Beecher."

"Why not?" Beecher was putting the rope around his waist.

"A tree smashed it."

Beecher was cold, and he knew he didn't have the strength left to carry both Rachael and Maddie up the mountain to his cabin. "Get on my back again. We're going to shoot for the Tea Room. It's an easier walk."

Maddie put her hands on his shoulders and poked her feet through the rope. She reached around his neck and shouted, "Up, Beech!"

Beecher covered Rachael's face with a flap of the blanket and lifted her into his arms. He started down the trail toward the main road, a trail only he knew in his mind. "Be my eyes, Maddie!" he called, turning his face. "If we can get out of the woods without falling on our faces, we'll be fine."

Maddie studied the ground in front of them. "Go for it, Beech," she called. "We got to get Mama to a warm place."

Beecher moved at a good speed, confident as he was in his knowledge of the land, and soon he was at the bridge's abutment.

Maddie directed him up onto the main road, then buried her face against his back. Out in the open the wind was fierce, and the blowing snow and sleet felt as if it were biting her skin. She could not imagine how Beecher could stand it. But Beecher Whitman had his mind set, and it wouldn't change until he had reached his goal, blizzard or no blizzard....

Tom Spinner was just about to open the door to leave when Doc Spangler entered the Tea Room. The old doctor shook the snow off his coat at the door and pulled the scarf from around his neck. He remembered his hat and slapped it across his thighs. "Well, I haven't seen one like this for a good long while," he said as he set his bag down on the counter and moved over to the stove.

Everyone in the room spoke. Besides Tom and Jim Gresby, there were Jim's wife, Betty, and Paul Tanner.

Betty was eating her supper behind the counter near the radio. "I didn't see you drive up, Doc," she said. "Where's your car?"

Doc waved his hand in disgust. "Drove the blasted thing into a snowdrift." He poured himself a cup of coffee and sat down in Lemus' chair beside the stove. He sniffed the air a few times. "Has Billy Gump been in here?"

Jim laughed. "Yesterday."

Doc shook his head.

Tom spoke up, "Doc, you're more than welcome to stay the night with us. No need to get caught in another drift."

"You sure, Tom? Don't want to put you young folks out any. How's that little boy?" Doc took a sip from his coffee cup.

"Oh, he's fine, Doc. And you won't be any trouble at all."

Paul Tanner finished his soda and placed the bottle in a wooden crate beside the drink box. "Everything's 'bout shut down, I reckon." He walked over to the counter and grimaced at the plate of fried chicken livers Jim was eating.

"Why you out so late, Doc?" Jim licked his fingers and reached into a basket for a buttered roll.

"Bud Newby's down with the gout, and he was wantin' somethin' to ease his misery." Doc stretched his arm out and felt the heat from the wood stove with one hand as he spoke. "Been with Joe and Anna Mae Brown over in Cow Hollow most of the day, though. Anna Mae gave birth to a seven-pound baby girl at 'bout 2:30 this afternoon." The old doctor reared back in his chair and pulled his watch out of his vest pocket. It was three minutes after seven o'clock.

Betty got up from her chair and began collecting Jim's dishes, and putting them with her own. "How is everybody over there?"

Doc put his watch away. "Oh, they're doing good. Thought Anna Mae might have a little trouble, but the baby came along just fine. No trouble at all."

Betty smiled. "Good. How many children do they have now?"

"This is their fifth," Doc chuckled, "and they're all girls. Think Joe is going to keep trying 'til he gets a farm hand in the bunch."

Tom looked out the store window. He watched as the windswept snow pushed across the lot. Paul Tanner's flatbed truck was parked on the opposite side of the gas pumps. Its windshield and hood were blanketed with snow and its motor was running. His own pickup truck was parked close to the front porch of the store. Sleet bounced off the passenger's window. He had left the truck's engine running and the heater on. Snow clung to the sides of the vehicle, and he noticed that his chained tire tracks leading into the lot were filling up with snow and sleet. He looked past the lights and the gas pumps into the darkness. "Well, I don't guess the Angel Carver will be leaving a package at the Browns' on a night like this," he said.

No one said anything for a minute.

Jim glanced over at Paul. "You seen anything of Rachael and the little one today, Paul?"

Paul shook his head. "We was hopin' they'd come on down, but I reckon they decided to stay up there." He rubbed the side of his face with his hand and looked up at the clock on the wall.

Then Doc spoke up, "The Browns been visited four times already. There's four of the prettiest carved angels on a shelf in their parlor I've ever seen. And I've seen a lot of 'em."

Betty placed the dishes gently in a split oak basket and tucked linen napkins around them. "Don't see how anyone could see to get around on a night like this."

Tom looked over at Paul Tanner. "Maybe the Angel Carver doesn't have to see."

Paul rapped his knuckles on the counter top, placed a nickel in Jim's hand for a pack of Nabs he'd picked up and put in his coat pocket. He smiled at Tom. "Tom, I got a feelin' that you want somebody to just come right out and say somethin', don't you?"

Tom shook his head and grinned. He looked over at Jim, who dropped Paul's nickel in the money tray of his big cash register. "Well, I've been around here long enough to know that folks are mighty protective of their own," he admitted. "I'm starting to get that way myself. Besides, if word got out about its being a certain individual, his way of life might be interrupted by news people and folks wanting to gawk at him."

Betty looked at her husband and winked. "That's right, Tom," she agreed. "And there's nobody 'round here that's sure who does them angels, anyway."

Paul Tanner had listened to the talk around him, but he hadn't spoken. Instead, he thought about the narrow road that wound its way up the mountain to his daughter's house. It would be covered with snow now, but he was sure his truck could make the trek. "Stubborn" worked two ways in the Tanner family, and if Rachael was bound and determined to weather out the storm on the mountain, her father was bent on talking her into coming down, if not for her and Maddie's own safety, then for his and Edna's peace of mind.

He was about to ask Tom if he'd consider a trip up the mountain with him when he stepped over to the window at the front of the store and strained his eyes to see past the light of the gas pumps. There was something moving out of sync with the wind and snow at the far reaches of the light. At first he thought it was an animal. Perhaps someone's cow had gotten loose. He put his face closer to the window and looked harder. "What the—" he started.

Jim and Betty looked out the window.

Betty put her hand to her mouth and gasped. "Oh, merciful heavens, Jim, somebody's been hurt!"

Doc stood up, and Tom followed Paul as he rushed out the front door.

By now, the figure of a man carrying a large bundle in his arms had walked into the light that shone over the gas pumps.

Paul jumped down from the porch and met the man lumbering across the lot. It was Beecher Whitman.

"God, Beecher, what in the world?" he shouted.

Beecher stopped. His face was wet with snow, but the brim of his hat and his eyebrows were frozen. His shirt and pants were also frozen and caked with snow. His hands were almost white. He tried to speak, but could only slur the name of Rachael.

Paul pried a frozen flap of the blanket back and saw his daughter's face. He took her from Beecher's cradled arms.

"Where's Maddie?" he shouted as he turned toward the Tea Room.

Tom grasped Beecher's bent arms and began guiding him to the store. He saw the little girl poke her head up over the big man's shoulder, and he called to Paul, "He's got her on his back!"

Jim Gresby held the door wide open as Paul carried Rachael in. Tom followed with Beecher and Maddie.

Betty had already run to the back of the store and pulled new blankets off the shelves. She spread one out on the pool table and shook the others out of their folds.

Doc grabbed his bag off the front counter and began to call out orders. "Paul, lay Rachael down on the table back there. Tom, you get that child off Beecher's back."

Doc moved quickly around Beecher and back to where Paul was prying the frozen blanket from around his daughter. He felt Rachael's neck and then her wrist. Her clothes were wet, but not frozen. He placed a hand on Paul's shoulder. "Paul, you help with your granddaughter. Betty's got to help me get this girl dry and warm."

Rachael moved her head and looked up at her father. Betty was already unbuttoning her wet blouse and Doc was removing her shoes. Paul bent down and kissed her with tears in his eyes. "It's going to be all right, baby," he promised. He held her hand in his. It was so cold. He could see dark bruises along her rib cage as Betty pulled back her blouse.

"Paul, let me get this off." Betty had no choice but to move between the father and daughter.

Reluctantly, Paul turned away from Rachael and focused on Maddie, who was sitting in the chair beside the stove. She had already slipped out of Beecher's big coat, her wet shoes, and her bib overalls. Jim had wrapped a blanket around her and was pouring hot water from a kettle that sat on the stove into a pan of cold water. He coaxed her to place her feet in the warm mixture, then turned to Beecher, who stood beside Tom at the counter. "Beecher, I got some clothes in the back for you to get into. Come along." He hurried around the pool table to a shelf which contained clothing merchandise. Tom guided Beecher back as Paul knelt in front of Maddie.

The little girl flung her arms around his neck and cried. "Is Mama going to be all right?"

Paul stroked her cheek and rubbed her back. He kissed his granddaughter on the forehead and reassured her, "She's going to be all right, Maddie. Don't you worry."

Maddie buried her face in the nook of his warm neck and cried, "I was so scared, Papa. The wind blew a tree down on the house, and Mama came and pulled me out of my window."

Paul closed his eyes and sighed. Guilt stung his heart, for he knew without being told that it must have been the old chestnut that had fallen, the one he'd been meaning to cut down for 'way too long.

Maddie whimpered and sniffled as she told her story. "Then we tried to come down the mountain, but the car slid off the road and turned over in the creek. There was water coming in, and Mama was stuck and sent me to get Beecher."

Tom returned to the front of the store. "Is there anything I can do, Paul?" he asked quietly.

Paul turned his head and looked up at the young man. "Yes, Tom. You got chains on your tires, don't you?"

"Sure do."

"Could you drive to the house and bring Edna here?"

Tom was putting on his coat as Paul spoke. "I'll have her here in a few minutes." He stepped out of the Tea Room and made his way to his truck.

Paul pulled the blanket back and examined Maddie's arms and legs. There wasn't a bruise or a cut on her. He was amazed after what she had been through.

"You seem to be fit as a fiddle." He tucked the blanket around her and hugged her.

117

Maddie touched her grandfather's face. "I prayed, Papa," she said. "I prayed that I could find Beecher's house, and when I got so cold and tired, I prayed that he would come and get me. When I couldn't walk anymore, a voice that sounded like Mama's told me to call him, and I did, Papa. And he heard me, and he came."

Paul swallowed hard, but couldn't hold back his tears. He cradled the little girl in his arms.

Maddie wasn't finished. She spoke quietly in his ear as he embraced her. "He put me on his back, Papa. Then we found the car, and Beecher had to turn it over and get Mama out."

Paul rubbed his eyes and pulled back from the girl. He studied her face. "He turned it over?" Paul looked toward the back of the room.

Doc raised up from Rachael and looked across the room at her father. He smiled and nodded his head. "We got us some fractured ribs, bruises and a minor concussion," he called, "but, all in all, I think she's going to be fine. Sore, but fine."

Betty was rubbing Rachael's feet and calling for Jim to bring another blanket.

Beecher had dressed in corduroy pants, a thick flannel shirt, and leather boots. He followed Jim to the pool table and stood there quietly.

The front door of the store flew open, and Edna Tanner came in with a bundle of clothes under her arm and Tom just behind her. She went straight to Maddie, kissed and hugged her, and gave her some socks and a shirt.

Paul related what he knew of the accident to his wife. Then the two of them went to Rachael's side.

Doc was about to give her a shot of something. "I've bound her ribs," he said. There was a bandage around her head, also. "She's got a cut on the back of her head and a minor concussion. We've got her warm, now, but what she needs is rest." A clear liquid spurted from the end of the needle he held in his hand. "Now, everybody say what you want to say to her, because she'll be asleep in a few minutes."

"Can we take her home, Doc?" Edna stroked the cheek of her daughter and held her hand.

"Tomorrow, Edna," he replied, looking over at Jim and Betty. "If you folks don't mind, we'll just let her sleep right here tonight."

"We don't mind at all, Doc." Jim leaned forward against the end of the pool table.

Betty nodded in agreement.

When Maddie had dressed, Tom walked with her to the pool table. He stood next to Jim and watched as the girl walked around and took her mother's hand. "I did it, Mama," she said. "I heard you tell me to call him, and I did it. He heard me, Mama. Beecher heard me."

A weak smile formed on Rachael's lips. She nodded her head slightly. "I knew you could do it, Maddie," she whispered.

Maddie kissed her mother and stood next to Beecher. She locked her small hands around his hand and leaned against him.

Rachael saw it and was at peace. She looked at

her parents and spoke softly. "I've been so foolish," she confided tearfully, "and it almost cost me—"

Edna quieted her. "Now, honey, we're all right here, and you and Maddie are safe. Don't blame yourself for an accident."

"But I could have lost her."

Paul bent down and looked his daughter in the eyes. "And I should have cut that chestnut tree three years ago." He squeezed her hand. "Let's not fret over 'could've' or 'should've.' Let's just be thankful you all are all right. Now you need to rest."

Paul and Edna stood back and Doc gave Rachael the shot. She closed her eyes slowly and opened them again.

"Beech?," she looked at the man standing tall beside her daughter.

"Yes, Rachael," he answered.

Maddie guided him to her mother's side.

Rachael reached out and took his hand. She pulled him close to her and spoke. Her voice was weak. "My house is gone, Beech. But I still want to live up on the mountain. I want to live with you."

Maddie looked at her grandparents and smiled, then put her hand on Beecher's arm.

The man's voice was full of emotion when he spoke. "But, Rachael, I'm just a scarred-up old blind relic."

Rachael placed a finger on his lips and quieted him. She looked upon his face and beyond his eyes and the scars of his past, and she saw the gentle spirit of the man she loved. "I love you, Beecher Whitman, and I would be your wife, if you would have me."

She touched his weathered cheek. "Life is such a precious gift and far too short to deny one's self of what is true." She kissed his hand. "I have been your eyes for almost all of my life, but it is you who allowed me to truly see."

Beecher placed his cheek next to hers and whispered in her ear. No one who stood around the pool table could hear his words. But Maddie knew what he said. She knew it in her heart.

Soon Rachael was asleep. Beecher sat in a chair at her side and held her hand.

Doc left with Tom, telling the Tanners that he'd return first thing in the morning to check on Rachael. Edna walked across the yard with Jim and Betty for the comfort of their guest bed. But Maddie stayed at the Tea Room with her grandfather, mother, and Beecher. Paul spoiled her and fed her Nabs and soda into the night.

Later that night as Beecher dozed in his chair beside Rachael, Paul asked Maddie a question. It had been on his mind all evening. "Honey, you said that after you and Beecher found the car, he turned it back over."

Maddie was tired and sat in her grandfather's lap, her head against his chest. "He did, Papa, but he wasn't alone." She played with a button on his shirt.

"What do you mean, he wasn't alone?" Paul cocked his head and looked at Maddie's face.

Without blinking an eye, she answered, "He tried to do it once by himself, but couldn't. Then he asked me to pray for him to have the strength to do it, and

I did. He prayed, too, and when he went back to the car, I saw some people around him."

"People?"

"Well, I don't know, 'cause it was dark, but I could see them in the water with him."

"Where did they come from?"

"I don't know. They were just there."

"How many were there?"

Maddie didn't hesitate in her answer. "Twelve," she said.

A chill ran over Paul Tanner as he considered what Maddie had said.

The little girl continued, "I know it was twelve 'cause when Beech got Mama out of the car and laid her on the blanket, they came and stood around us. That's when I counted them. It was easier to count them in the snow, up close."

"What did they look like? Did you know them?"

Maddie thought for a moment. "I never saw their faces, but I wasn't afraid of them 'cause they were helping Beech."

"What do you mean?"

"The car had lots of water in it and Mama was pinned on her back. I thought she'd drowned 'cause she was so cold and wasn't breathing or moving when Beech laid her down on the blanket. But Beech said she was waiting, and he told me to call her back. We both did. And when Beech was pushing on Mama's chest and blowing air into her mouth, those people were putting their hands on him and touching Mama's head."

Paul looked over at Beecher. "Are you sure of this, Maddie?" he asked.

The girl nodded her head. "I don't know who they were, Papa, but I know they were there, and they walked with us until I saw the lights at the gas pumps."

"Which way did they go then?"

"I don't know. They just weren't there any more." Maddie sat up and studied her grandfather's face. "You believe me, don't you, Papa?" she asked.

Paul pushed a strand of her disheveled hair out of her face. "Yes, honey," he answered, "I believe you." Quietly he walked her over to the pool table, lifted her up and let her crawl over next to her mother. He pulled a blanket over her and kissed her. "God bless," he whispered.

"Goodnight, Papa."

Paul put a couple of short logs in the wood stove and sat back down in his chair. He thought long into the night about Beecher Whitman and Rachael and how hearts are brought together. He thought about what Maddie had told him, and just before he fell asleep, he realized he was at peace with it all.

Sometime during the night he was vaguely aware of the sound of the wind and the closing of a door, but the sound was distant as if in a dream.

In the wee hours before dawn, the sound came to him again. This time, he awakened and opened his eyes. He leaned forward in his chair and looked across the room. There he saw a man placing a neatly wrapped brown package on the table next to

Rachael's head. He kissed her temple lightly, then turned and quietly moved to the side door of the store. Paul watched in silence.

The man put his hand on the door knob and turned it, but before he pulled open the door, he turned his face to Paul.

Paul stood up and spoke. "Thank you, Beecher. Thank you for bringing them out of the storm."

Beecher smiled, then opened the door and stepped out into the darkness. By the time daylight came, his footprints had disappeared in the snow....

On a sunny April day in 1940, a flatbed truck made its way up the narrow mountain road above Silver Creek. It paused at a steep driveway that led up a finger ridge, then continued over a rise and around a long bend in the road. When the driver applied the brakes and stopped at his destination, he cut off the ignition and turned to his passenger.

Edna Tanner reached over and grasped her husband's hand. "They're happy up here with him, aren't they, Paul?"

The front door of the big cabin swung open and Maddie ran out on the porch. Beecher and Rachael followed her.

The little girl hurried over to the truck and reached deep into the breast pocket of her faded bib overalls. Paul opened the truck door and greeted her with a kiss.

"Look what I have," Maddie was bubbling as she pulled out a baby squirrel. "His name is Mr. Doodle," she announced as the critter ran up her arm and onto her shoulder.

Edna laughed, "Well, I'll be. Look at that!" She got down from the truck and lifted a pie and a jar of honey off the seat, then walked to the cabin.

Paul said "Hello" to Mr. Doodle, then walked with Maddie up on the porch.

A gentle breeze played with the line of wind chimes as they greeted one another.

Maddie chased a chipmunk around the corner of the cabin as Rachael and Edna stepped into the great room, chatting.

Paul leaned against the porch rail and looked out through the woods. The tree limbs were alive with new foliage, and flowering wild dogwoods were scattered throughout the hollow like ragged white lace. The shadows of the hemlocks along the creek danced into the shining leaves of mountain laurel and lent mystery to the forest undergrowth.

"By golly, Beecher, it's mighty fine up here."

Beecher breathed in a full chest of air. "That it is, Paul," he agreed.

Maddie ran up on the porch and swerved into the house. The smell of biscuits and fried chicken wafted through the doorway as Rachael walked out and stepped between the two men. "Dinner is ready, you two," she said while ushering them into the cabin. Her smile was fetching. Her happiness was apparent.

The door closed behind them, and as with the nature of spring, life began anew in Beecher's Hollow....

Christmas Day 1998

When Julianna awoke, she was surprised that she had fallen asleep in her grandmother's chair. She rubbed her eyes, stretched her arms, and yawned. She looked for the book she had read the night before, but it was not there. The picture album was on the table where her grandmother had left it, but the book was gone. Puzzled, Julianna stood up and searched the floor to see if it had fallen off the chair.

She opened the picture album and flipped through the stiff pages. She studied old photographs she had never paid much attention to until now. There were pictures of her grandmother as a child, alone and with her mother. Names written in ink were now familiar. Her great-grandparents stood smiling in a yard with a wood shed and a small river behind them. A little girl dressed in overalls fed a bread crumb to a bushy-tailed squirrel perched on her shoulder, Julianna turned the page and found the picture of a man standing on the porch of a log cabin. He wore round, dark glasses and had a kind smile. He was a powerful-looking man. She tried to count the many wind chimes which hung along the eaves of the porch. Next, she studied a picture of the man with a woman and a child standing together on the porch. The next few pages contained all of these people in various stages of their lives. The last picture in the album was of Julianna's grandmother as a young woman, alone. Beneath this photograph, there was written one word: "Believe."

Julianna looked up then, and for the first time, noticed the gifts which had been placed around the Christmas tree. She heard a giggle and the shuffling of slippers on the staircase in the foyer. She closed the picture album as both Will and Missy scurried into the room. They barely noticed her as they raced to the tree and tore into their presents. Soon her mother and father and grandparents entered the room, and there was laughter and talk and pretty paper and ribbons everywhere. Christmas music played over the stereo speakers, and after it was all over, Julianna helped her mother and father clean up the mess and straighten up around the tree while her grandparents prepared breakfast.

Will and Missy had practically abandoned reality for that wonderful state of child mind known as toy land. They were both precious and wild, their eyes full of sparkle.

After breakfast Julianna walked up the stairs to her room. Being the oldest grandchild, she had laid claim to her own bedroom at her grandparents' home. It was small and contained a single twin bed and table, a chest of drawers with a mirror, and an old beanbag chair. The room had once been used as her grandfather's tax office.

When she entered the room, she walked to the chest of drawers and pulled open the top one. She chose a pair of dark blue jeans and a maroon turtleneck and laid them on top of the chest. She looked at herself in the mirror and pushed back her hair. That's when she saw the package bound with beige string. It was on her bedside table. She walked around the foot of the bed, picked up the package, and sat down. The string was tied in a single bow, and someone had written her name beside it with a pencil.

Julianna felt her heart beat faster as she untied the string and carefully unfolded the edges and corners of the paper. When she saw the gift, she was filled with wonder. She touched the smooth wings of an angel and traced the contours of its body with her finger. She thought about the story she had read and recalled the photograph of the man in her grandmother's album.

"It is beautiful, isn't it, Julianna?"

Julianna turned her head and smiled at her grandmother. "Oh, yes, Gramma, it is!" she answered. "I loved the story."

The woman walked over and sat down beside the girl. "Miracles are like the stars to one who believes.

They are endless." She hugged Julianna and looked at the angel. "He would've wanted you to have it."

A voice called from downstairs. It was Julianna's grandfather. "Madison? Maddie, you up there?"

"I'll be right down," she answered, patting Julianna on the leg. She got up and walked toward the door.

"Gramma?"

"Yes, dear." Maddie turned around.

Julianna set the angel on the table and touched the tip of one of its wings. "What was he like?" she asked.

Maddie smiled through her tears. "Oh, he was a wonderful man, Julianna, and he loved me as his own."

"Was your mother happy?"

Maddie clasped her hands and brought them up under her chin. She looked away for a moment and felt a twinge of longing enter her heart. "Always, dear," she answered with a smile. "She was always happy with him." Maddie turned and walked out of the room.

Julianna looked again at the beautiful angel. She clasped her hands behind her head and lay back on her bed. That's when she felt something on the bedspread tucked beneath her pillow. She reached back and felt the corner of a book. Smiling, she pulled it out and looked at it. It was her grandmother's story. She laid it over her heart and closed her eyes. "I believe," she whispered. "I believe."

The End

Titles by Francis Eugene Wood

The Wooden Bell (A Christmas Story)
The Legend of Chadega and the Weeping Tree
Wind Dancer's Flute
The Crystal Rose
The Angel Carver
The Fodder Milo Stories
The Nipkins (Trilogy)
Snowflake (A Christmas Story)
The SnowPeople
Return to Winterville
Winterville Forever
Autumn's Reunion (A Story of Thanksgiving)
The Teardrop Fiddle
Two Tales and a Pipe Dream
The Christmas Letter
Tackle Box Memories
Moonglow
Sunflower
The Keeper of the Tree

These books are available through the author's
website: www.tipofthemoon.com
Email address: fewwords@moonstar.com

Write to:
Tip-of-the-Moon Publishing Company
175 Crescent Road
Farmville, Virginia 23901

Author Francis Eugene Wood writes his stories from his
home in Buckingham County, Virginia. He is known for
his rich descriptions of rural Virginia life and his unique
ability to blend fact and fiction in a way that mirrors the
world around him. The award-winning author has been
called "imaginative," "prolific," and a "natural storyteller."
His books are released through Tip-of-the-Moon Publishing Company, a company he owns and operates with
his wife, Chris.